INTO THE FIELD GUIDE

A Walk in the Woods

By Emily Laber-Warren

downtown bookworks

ABOUT THE AUTHOR

Emily Laber-Warren is director of the health and science reporting program at the City University of New York Graduate School of Journalism. She is also the mother of twin boys who love to explore.

AUTHOR'S ACKNOWLEDGMENTS

I'd like to offer a great big thank you to the following consultants for taking the time to share their knowledge and expertise with me:

Erin Allen, K–12 education outreach coordinator, School of Natural Resources and Environment, University of Michigan; Bree Benton Arthur, education director, LandPaths, Santa Rosa, California; Anna Brunner, conservation biology master's student, University of Michigan; Kath Buffington, environmental educator, Rochester, New York; Peter Leveque, retired biology instructor, Santa Rosa Junior College; Frederique Lavoipierre, entomology outreach program coordinator, Sonoma State University Field Stations & Nature Preserves; Maree Mitchell, science teacher, Missoula, Montana; David Moskowitz, wildlife photographer, tracker, and consultant; Dr. John Perrine, associate curator, of mammals, California Polytechnic State University; Tobias Policha, director, Institute of Contemporary Ethnobotany, Eugene, Oregon; Dr. Scott Sink, professor of silviculture, California Polytechnic State University; Dr. Philip Stouffer, ornithologist, Louisiana State University; Dawn Stover, science and environmental writer; Dr. Tom A. Titus, herpetology instructor, University of Oregon.

Dedicated to two young naturalists, Nathaniel and Jeremy.

downtown bookworks

Design by Georgia Rucker

Printed in China, January 2013

ISBN 978-1-935703-26-6

10 9 8 7 6 5 4 3 2 1

Downtown Bookworks Inc.
285 West Broadway
New York, NY 10013
www.dtbwpub.com

Contents

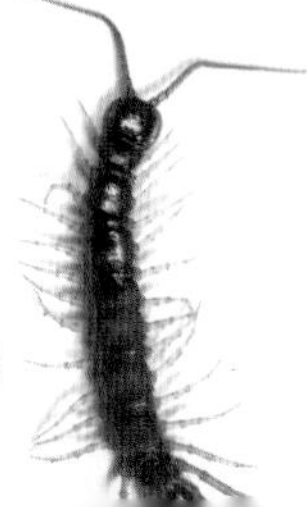

Secrets of the Forest

Take a walk in the woods. What do you see? Trees. Bushes. The path ahead. It might seem quiet and still. But there is life all around you if you know where to look. The forest is full of clues.

SEE A LINE OF HOLES IN A TREE TRUNK?
They may have been made by a **woodpecker.**

IS THERE A TRAIL OF SLIME ON LEAVES?
Perhaps a **banana slug** just came by.

MOVE A ROCK. WHAT'S UNDERNEATH?
Perhaps a pill bug or a **salamander.**

HEAR A MUSICAL, WHISTLING CALL?
There could be a gorgeous red **cardinal** right above you.

This book will teach you the names of some of the plants

and animals you are likely to see in the woods. Knowing their names, you may see them differently. A leaf won't be just any leaf. You'll know that **oak** leaves are lacy and **cottonwood** leaves are triangular. **Maple** leaves are shaped like hands. **Sweetgum** leaves are star shaped.

NATURE FINDS

As you look more carefully, you'll start to find cool things: feathers, butterfly wings, acorns, empty cocoons, pine cones, and more. Each is beautiful in its own way. Put them in your collecting box. When you get home, examine your finds with your magnifying glass. Label them, saying where and when you found each one.

Keep taking walks in the woods. Each time, you will learn more.

A FEW THINGS TO REMEMBER

1. **Never harm anything.** Don't uproot plants. Don't bring wild animals home.
2. **Be careful.** Look out for poison ivy and poison oak. (See page 23.) Make sure you wash your hands when you get home.
3. **Follow the rules.** Some state parks do not allow you to take anything away.
4. **Take a grown-up with you,** unless you know the area well and have permission to go alone.

Plants and Fungi

Life on earth is made possible because of something extraordinary that plants do. They build themselves out of practically nothing. Plants take sunlight, water, and a few ingredients from the air and soil and turn them into energy. They use this energy to grow. The process is called photosynthesis. They also store energy in their leaves and fruits, which is why snacking on bananas or nuts gives you an energy boost.

Some animals eat plants. Some animals eat animals that eat plants. However you slice it, plants are the most important food there is.

In this section, you'll learn about many different kinds of plants: trees, flowers, mosses, and ferns. You'll also find out about mushrooms. Mushrooms aren't plants, but they aren't animals, either. They belong to a group of living things called fungi.

Oak Trees

Oaks are among the biggest and most beautiful trees you will see in the forest. The biggest ones may be hundreds of years old.

White oak

Red oak

OAK FAMILIES

Most oak trees have leaves that are long and lacy. They all produce acorns. But not all oak trees are the same. Pick up an oak leaf. Run your finger along the outline of the leaf. Are its edges smooth and rounded? If so, this tree belongs to the **white oak** group. If its edges are pointy, the tree belongs to the **red oak** group.

FIELD FACT An oak tree will not produce an acorn until it is at least 20 years old.

ACORNS

Every summer, an oak tree makes thousands of acorns. Acorns are seeds that can grow into new oak trees. But they don't often get the chance. Birds, chipmunks, and squirrels break open the hard shells of acorns to eat the delicious nuts inside.

Like the cans of food on your kitchen shelves, acorns last a long time without spoiling. Many animals save acorns in special hiding places so that during the winter they will have good things to eat. Sometimes, an animal forgets where it has left some of its acorns. Instead of being eaten, those acorns may become new trees.

NATURE FINDS

EXAMINING ACORNS

Pick up an acorn. Before putting it in your collecting box, look carefully. Is it shiny or bumpy? Is its hat rough or smooth? How much of the acorn does the hat cover? Half? A third? Or does it sit flat on top like a beret? Try to gather as many types of acorns as you can. Each one comes from a different kind of oak tree.

Red oak

White oak

Black oak

California live oak

Maple Trees

In the fall, if the trees around you turn yellow, orange, and red, chances are that some of them are maples.

Maple trees are most common in the Northeast, which is famous for its fall colors.

MAPLE LEAVES

Even before fall comes, maple trees are easy to spot because they have hand-shaped leaves, with five points instead of fingers. Unlike oak leaves, which climb their branches one by one, maple leaves grow in pairs, one directly across from the other.

Samara

"HELICOPTER" SEEDS

Every kind of tree makes its own seed. Oaks have acorns. Maples have **samaras.** Samaras are so light and well balanced that when they fall off the tree they spin in perfect circles, like a helicopter propeller. Hold a maple samara over your head, drop it, and see for yourself.

TREE SAP FOR BREAKFAST?

If you've ever had maple syrup on your pancakes, then you know another special thing about maple trees. Maple syrup comes from a liquid inside trees called sap. Just as blood travels around your body, bringing energy to your arms, legs, and head, sap carries energy to the different parts of the tree.

Sap is collected in late winter or early spring.

Farmers make small holes in the trunks of maple trees so that some of the sap drips out. Buckets attached to the trees collect the sap. Sap isn't delicious enough to pour on your pancakes. It tastes like bland sugar water. Farmers boil the sap for many hours until it gets thick and sweet enough for syrup or candy. It takes about 40 quarts of sap to make 1 quart of maple syrup.

Evergreens

In the winter, oak and maple leaves die, but evergreens stay green. These trees have small, needle-like leaves that don't fall off in cold weather.

TREES WITH POINTY NEEDLES

There are many kinds of pine trees, including the **white pine,** which grows in the eastern part of the United States, and the **ponderosa pine,** which grows out west. The needles of pine trees grow together in bundles. Count how many are in a bundle to help discover what kind of pine you are looking at. The needles of white pines grow in bundles of five. Ponderosa pine needles grow in groups of three, or sometimes two.

Ponderosa pine

FIELD FACT Pine needles have a thick outer layer of wax that helps keep water inside the needle from evaporating. This helps pine trees survive in dry and cold seasons.

Colorado blue spruce

You can roll the needles of spruce trees between your fingers. If you see a **Colorado blue spruce,** give it a try.

Some people say that fir trees are "flat and friendly." Like "fir," those two words begin with an f, so they are easy to remember. What do people mean by this? The needles of fir trees, such as the **balsam fir,** are flat. And unlike pine or spruce needles, they are "friendly," meaning that they are not too sharp.

Balsam fir

NATURE FINDS

CREATING A CONE COLLECTION

The cones of evergreens are as different from one another as shells on a beach. The cone of the white pine is long and narrow. The cones of spruce trees are papery and easily crushed. The cone of the hemlock is tiny and as hard as a marble. The cone of the Douglas-fir has little forked streamers called bracts.

Spruce cones

Hemlock cones

Douglas-fir cones

White pine cones

More Evergreens

Eastern redcedar

Junipers, coast redwoods, and giant sequoias are other well-known evergreen trees.

Pines, spruces, and firs (see pages 12–13) have long, skinny needles, but other types of evergreens have small leaves that sometimes look almost as if they've been braided.

One of these is the **juniper.** There are a few kinds of juniper trees in the United States. One that grows in the eastern part of the country is the **eastern redcedar.** The needles at the tips of some branches—the newest ones—are pointy. But others crisscross to form smooth ropes.

Juniper needles

Juniper cones look like berries. They are small, round, and whitish blue. They are a favorite food of many birds.

Juniper cones

NATURE FINDS

SCRUNCH AND SNIFF

Break off a clump of redcedar needles and crush them with your fingernails. Now put your fingers to your nose. The redcedar has a strong smell. What do you think of it? Moths hate it! That's why people make closets and chests from this wood—to keep moths from eating holes in their clothes.

SUPERSIZE TREES

Coast redwoods are the tallest trees in the world. Scientists are discovering that there are certain earthworms, salamanders, and other animals that never, ever touch the ground. They spend their entire lives in the branches of redwoods!

Coast redwoods

Giant sequoia trees are not as tall as coast redwoods, but they are much thicker. Giant sequoias are the largest trees in the world. Their cones are tiny, though: only about 2 inches long.

Giant sequoia

Giant sequoia cones

FAIRY RINGS

In a redwood forest, you may come upon a group of trees in a perfect circle. These "fairy rings" form when an old redwood dies and young ones sprout from its roots. According to legend, elves and other creatures dance inside these magical spaces.

Fairy ring

Trees That Grow Near Water

All trees need water to live, but only a few kinds of trees are happy being wet all the time. These are the trees you are likely to find if you go walking near a pond, lake, or stream.

FLYING FLUFF BALLS

Cottonwood tree leaf

Cottonwood trees have triangle-shaped leaves and stems that are flat, not round. Because of their unusual shape, cottonwood leaves catch the slightest breeze. You will see and hear them fluttering on all but the calmest days.

During the months of May and June, cottonwood trees release lots of fluffy white seeds into the air. The seeds float through the air like tiny bits of cotton candy. In the fall, cottonwoods make a sticky resin that smells delicious. Bees use this resin to seal their hives.

Cottonwood tree

Cottonwood seeds

SECRETS OF BARK

Bark does for trees what our skin does for us. It protects them—from rain, snow, hungry insects, and other things. The bark of most trees is brown or gray. And the look of bark changes as a tree gets older. So it can be difficult to recognize trees from their bark. But a few trees that live near water have bark that is easy to spot.

Paper birch

The **paper birch,** or white birch, has white bark that peels off the tree all by itself. It looks as if the tree is making sheets of paper for you!

Sycamore

The trunks of **sycamore** trees are covered in greenish, yellowish, and cream-colored patches. That's because the bark is very thin and it flakes off, like peeling paint, showing different parts of the inner bark.

MAKE IT

GROW YOUR OWN WILLOW

Because they live near water, **willow trees** are prepared for floods. If a willow washes away, it can take root wherever it lands. In fact, willows sprout so easily that you can get one to grow in your kitchen. Just cut off part of a willow branch and place it in a glass vase or cup. Check it every day. Before you know it, you will see new roots forming. You can then plant your willow in a pot or the ground outside.

Willow branches

Fall Leaves

How do you know when winter is coming? The weather gets colder. And it is dark in the morning when you wake up to go to school.

Alder

Trees also know when winter is coming. Just as you trade your shorts and T-shirts for long pants and jackets, trees make changes, too.

In the winter, less sunlight hits the earth. This is a problem for trees because they use sunlight to make energy. So to prepare for winter, trees suck energy out of their leaves and store it in their trunks and roots. The green color disappears from their leaves. Other colors that had been hidden by the green—like yellow, red, and orange—now show through.

Fall leaves come in many shapes and colors. They are fun to collect. Here are some to look for.

Sweetgum

Oak
Sassafras
Tuliptree
Dogwood
Maple

All trees make flowers in the spring. But the flowers of most trees are hidden or are too small to see. Only a few trees have showy blossoms. Because these trees are so pretty, people plant them in their yards. But you may also find them growing wild.

SHOWY BLOSSOMS

One tree with a lovely flower is the **buckeye.** The buckeye's flowers cluster together. These clusters stick straught up from the tree's branches, like candles.

The actual flowers of the **dogwood** tree are the small greenish-yellow ones growing in the center. The four white "petals" are actually bracts, which are a type of leaf.

The **catalpa** tree has heart-shaped leaves. Its flowers are white or yellow, with deep holes inside, covered with little spots. Catalpa flowers turn into long, skinny capsules that hang down from the trees all winter. These capsules can be as long as your arm! Catalpa capsules are a great item to add to your collection.

Catalpa tree

Capsules

Catalpa flower

THE MARVELOUS MAGNOLIA

There are many kinds of **magnolia** trees, each with a different flower. Some are yellow, some are purple, and some are white, but most magnolia flowers are large and sweet smelling.

One of the most beautiful magnolia trees is the southern magnolia, which grows in the southeastern United States. It is the state flower of Mississippi.

FIELD FACT Magnolia trees grew on earth long before people existed. They were around in the days of the dinosaurs!

Southern magnolia tree

Magnolia flower

The First Blooms of Spring

Plants need energy to make flowers, and they get it from the sun. In the summer, when trees are covered with leaves, the forest floor is dark, so most forest wildflowers come out in April and May—to grab as much sunlight as they can before the trees regrow their leaves.

Trout lily

LOOKING DOWN

Springtime brings lots of rain. Flowers contain delicate parts that can be damaged by a hard shower. That's why many plants of early spring, such as the **trout lily,** face downward. They are protecting their precious flowers.

Mayapple

The leaves of the **mayapple** act just like an umbrella, sheltering the plant's white flower from rain. So search carefully in springtime for spots of color that may be hiding. The **jack-in-the-pulpit,** a strange flower that looks like a folded leaf, avoids the rain in a different way.

Jack-in-the-pulpit

Wherever you live, there is an early-blooming flower that people call **spring beauty.**

These spring beauty flowers grow in the eastern United States.

Trilliums are also known as wake-robins because they bloom around the same time that robins begin to appear in the spring.

Trillium

POISONOUS PLANTS

Not all spring plants are good to touch. Some have oils that may irritate your skin. Both **poison ivy** and **poison oak** can give people an itchy skin rash. Poison ivy grows only in the eastern half of the United States. Poison oak is found all over.

Poison ivy

The leaves of both plants grow in groups of three: two that face one another and a third that sticks out between them on a longer stem. The leaves of poison oak are shaped like the leaves of a white oak tree. Those of poison ivy are almond shaped. If you think you have touched one of these plants, wash with soap and water within 15 minutes to avoid getting the rash. Remember this saying: "Leaves of three, let it be."

Poison Oak

Summer Wildflowers

Once summer arrives, you will find lots of wildflowers at forest edges and in clearings.

Evening primroses

The **evening primrose** is a yellow flower whose blossoms open at sundown. Sit for a bit at the end of the day, and you can watch it happen!

Purple passionflower

The **purple passionflower,** also known as the maypop, grows on twisty vines in the southeastern United States. Its flower is so complex, it looks like something out of a Dr. Seuss book.

Lupines

If you come across a bunch of **lupines,** purple or pink flowers on tall stalks, squeeze one of the blossoms between your pointer finger and your thumb. It will open and close, like a mouth.

Columbine

Columbines come in different colors, but one common type looks like a fancy red bell with a yellow ringer inside.

Mariposa lily

There are many colors and kinds of **mariposa lilies.** This flower is as beautiful as a butterfly—which is what *mariposa* means in Spanish.

FIND THE SPOT

Queen Anne's lace did not grow in the United States until people brought it here from Europe.

From a distance it looks entirely white, but if you look carefully you'll notice a tiny red spot in the center. According to an old story, this is supposed to be the drop of blood that came from Queen Anne's finger when she pricked herself with a needle while making lace.

Queen Anne's lace

More Summer Wildflowers

Some wildflowers are more complicated than they appear. They are called composite flowers. What looks like just one flower is actually dozens or even hundreds of tiny flowers all living together.

Black-eyed Susan

Some of the most common wildflowers, such as the **black-eyed Susan,** are composites. Ask a grown-up to help you cut one straight down the middle lengthwise. Carefully remove one of the brown parts from the center without damaging it. This is a mini-flower, also known as a floret. The black-eyed Susan's yellow petals are a different kind of floret.

The **coneflower,** Echinacea, can be made into tea or an herbal remedy to ward off colds. It is also a composite.

Coneflower

Goldenrod is another composite flower. It grows all over the United States.

Goldenrod

FIELD FACT Many people think they are allergic to goldenrod, but other plants, like ragweed, are really what's making them sneeze.

Daisies and **dandelions** are composite flowers, too. When a dandelion turns into a puffball in late summer, each of its fluffy parachutes contains the seed of an individual flower.

Dandelion

MAKE IT

FLOWER PRESSING

If you press your flowers, they will stay colorful for years! You can turn pressed flowers into bookmarks, greeting cards, and other cool gifts. Flowers with thin petals, such as **buttercups,** are best for pressing.

Try to pick flowers on a dry day. Leave half an inch of stem attached. Place the flowers between two sheets of blank newsprint or printer paper, leaving space around each flower. Then put a sheet of cardboard on either side of the paper. Stack a few heavy books on top. A hot place, like an attic or the trunk of a car, is best. Small flowers will dry in five days. Larger flowers may take a week.

Pressed buttercups

FEATURE

The All-Important Seed

Often, we enjoy flowers for their scents and their beauty, and fruits for their delicious taste. But did you know that all flowers become fruits? Fruits hold the plant's seeds. And inside each seed is a new baby plant!

Apple blossoms

An **apple** tree makes flowers in the springtime. By the fall, those flowers have turned into apples. Have you ever noticed the little brown seeds inside an apple? If you planted those seeds instead of throwing them away, they might grow into new apple trees.

FIELD FACT Apples and pears are tasty, nutritious fruits, but there are plenty of fruits that aren't meant to be eaten by humans, like pinecones, acorns, and the helicopters of maple trees.

SPREADING SEEDS AROUND

Seeds must travel for plants to thrive. For example, an acorn that falls directly below its oak tree will not get enough sun to grow. But an acorn that is hidden by a squirrel in a meadow will have all the light it needs to grow into a large, new oak tree. Different fruits have different ways of helping their seeds travel far.

Cottonwood seeds

Dandelion

The fruits of **cottonwood** trees and **dandelions** hold seeds that are light and fluffy enough to float away on the wind. Plants such as **burdock** and **sticklewort** have burrs. Burrs get their seeds moving by hitching a ride on an animal's fur or on your clothes. The seeds of apples, peaches, and pears travel in a different way. Bears, raccoons, rabbits, and other animals eat them. Later, the seeds fall to the ground as part of the animals' poop!

FIELD FACT The man who invented Velcro came up with the idea after finding burrs stuck to himself and his dog after a walk.

Animals help spread seeds around.

Burdock

Sticklewort

NATURE FINDS

PROTECTIVE THORNS

The seeds of the **chestnut** tree live inside a protective, prickly burr. The thorns on the outside of the burr discourage animals from eating the burrs. When the seeds are ready to grow, the burr pops open.

Chestnut burr

Fruits, Fruits, Everywhere

Some fruits, like cherries, peaches, and apples, are familiar to us because we eat them. But many other fruits that are not good to eat are still cool to collect. Here are some of the fruits that you may find during your walks in the woods. How many you can find?

A vine called **bittersweet** makes orange berries with yellow caps that keep their color when they dry out.

The acorn is the oak tree's fruit.

The **sweetgum** tree makes a bristly round fruit.

Sassafras trees make long berry-like fruit.

When **milkweed** pods are mature, they burst open and release small brown seeds attached to white silky threads that scatter in the wind.

The samara is the fruit of the **maple**.

Ragweed plants make burrs.

The **hemlock** tree makes tiny cones.

Pines and **spruces** make large cones.

Wild Treats

Wild raspberries

As a rule, you should never eat berries you find in the woods. They might give you a tummy ache— or worse. But a few types of wild berries are delicious and perfectly safe. Learn to recognize them, and you'll be able to grab snacks on the go. Just remember: Before picking any berries, make sure a grown-up agrees that it's a good idea.

All berries like sun, so you will find them on the edges of woods.

Blackberries

Strawberries

Raspberry and **blackberry** bushes grow at least as tall as an 8-year-old and, at times, much higher. They are prickly, so be careful. You'll recognize the berries: tiny round parts form a thimble shape with a hole in the center. Unripe blackberries are red. They ripen in July and August and turn dark.

Wild **strawberries** grow close to the ground on plants whose leaves grow in threes. These fruits are as small as the tip of your finger, with tiny seeds on the outside—mini versions of the ones you see at the supermarket. They ripen all summer long.

Both wild **blueberries** and **huckleberries** look a lot like the blueberries we buy at the grocery store. They grow on bushes that can be as low as your waist or grow taller than an adult. They ripen from July to September.

Violet

FLOWERS AS FOOD

Did you know that some flowers are also good to eat? Some people cover **violets** in hard sugar and use them to decorate cakes. It's easier to just pick a few violets and sprinkle their petals over a fruit salad. You can also make or buy jelly made of rose petals. Try rose petal tea! All you need to do is boil a cup of wild rose petals in two cups of water for five minutes, then strain them and add honey. **Wild mustard** flowers have a spicy bite to them. Again, have a grown-up double-check before you eat anything you find outside.

Mustard flower

FEATURE

Chemicals in Nature

Hungry Japanese beetles can ruin crops and gardens. But one bite of a geranium, and the beetle falls into a coma.

Imagine you are a plant. Ah, you think, this is the life, soaking up the sun, taking it easy, no homework. Plants make their own food, so snacks arrive 24/7. . .

But wait! What if a beetle starts munching your leaves and you want to get away? Hey, you think, I can't move! Being stuck in one place is a serious problem for plants. But they have come up with some smart solutions.

Plants make many kinds of chemicals. For instance, some plants make chemicals that can paralyze hungry beetles. A stunned beetle will fall right off the plant's leaf.

As a caterpillar, a monarch eats only **milkweed,** which contains a poisonous chemical. The poison remains even after the caterpillar becomes a butterfly. This is why many animals do not eat monarchs.

A monarch butterfly rests on milkweed.

A hummingbird visits a trumpet vine flower.

THE BIRDS AND THE BEES

Plants make sweet chemicals, too. That's why their flowers smell so nice. These smells and the flowers' bright colors attract animals such as bees, butterflies, and hummingbirds.

Every flower has a shape that invites a particular animal partner. For example, **trumpet vine** flowers are deep, to make room for a hummingbird's long beak. And **snapdragons** have a "landing pad" for bees. The flowers open only when a bee of just the right size lands on them! These animals find a delicious liquid inside the flowers. It is called nectar.

A bee extends its tongue to drink the nectar of a snapdragon.

ANIMALS HELPING PLANTS

While they are drinking the nectar, the butterflies, bees, and birds brush against other parts of the flower. Something called pollen sticks to them and rubs off when they visit other flowers. When pollen from one flower reaches another flower, the result is a seed—the beginnings of a new plant. In this way, animals help plants survive and spread to new places.

Ferns and Mosses

Tucked away in the shadiest spots of the forest are some of the oldest plants on earth. Ferns and mosses grew here before there were any animals, flowers, or trees.

Ferns and mosses are different from other plants because they don't have seeds. Instead, they have tiny bundles of powder called **spores.** This dust floats in the wind. When conditions are right, the spores land and grow into new plants.

A fern leaf is called a frond. Turn over a fern frond and you may see lots of tiny dots. These are spores ready to burst.

Baby ferns are called **fiddleheads** because they look like the curly tip of a violin. In the spring, you may see fiddleheads poking out of the ground. As ferns grow, their leaves unroll and spread out.

Often you can tell what kind of fern you are looking at by the shape of its leaves. A **sensitive fern** has broad, flat leaves. It gets its name from the fact that it withers at the first sign of frost. The leaves of the **Christmas fern** stay green

all year long. An **ostrich fern**'s fronds resemble the frilly tail feathers of an ostrich.

The **bracken fern** has triangular leaves. This fern makes chemicals that repel insects. When you're out walking, carry a bracken fern frond to help keep the mosquitoes away!

A CUSHION FOR YOUR FEET

When **pincushion moss** is dry, it is brown and brittle. But when the weather is wet, it sucks up water like a sponge and becomes deep green and very soft.

Sphagnum moss grows in swamps called bogs. Grab a handful and squeeze. Notice how much water it holds. Throughout history, this moss has come in handy. Nurses wrapped soldiers' wounds in bandages made of this supersoft moss. Mothers used sphagnum as bedding for mattresses and cribs. They even diapered their babies with it!

Mushrooms

Amanita mushroom

A mushroom is not a plant. It is a fungus. Actually, it is part of a fungus. Most of the fungus is made up of long, stringy hairlike parts growing underground. Think of mushrooms as fruit growing on a "tree" hidden underground.

A fungus has an important job. It is like a small, natural recycling center. It breaks dead leaves and insects into tiny, tiny pieces. These small bits return to the soil. New plants grow out of the healthy soil created by the mushrooms.

MUSHROOMS ON THE MOVE

When a fungus is ready to spread, it sends up a mushroom. The mushroom makes lots of spores, which look like dust. The wind helps to spread the spores around. Just as seeds can turn into new plants, spores can become new fungi.

Mushrooms come in many cool shapes. Enjoy looking at them, but remember: *Never eat a wild mushroom. It may be poisonous.*

Jack-o'-lantern mushrooms are orange, but at night, they glow in the dark! These mushrooms are poisonous.

POISONOUS

Jack-o'-lantern mushroom

The **amanita mushroom** has a bright red, umbrella-shaped cap. Sometimes the cap has white dots on it. This mushroom is also poisonous.

Shelf fungi

The **shelf fungus** gets its name because it is flat and sticks straight out from trees. It eats wood.

SPORE ART

Some mushrooms have delicate veins underneath their caps. These are called gills. In many mushrooms, the spores develop in the gills. Remove a mushroom's stem and place its cap on a piece of paper, gills facing down. Cover the cap with an upside-down glass or bowl. Leave it overnight. In the morning, carefully remove the mushroom. The spores will have fallen to the paper, creating a lovely design. Scientists can use spore prints to tell one kind of mushroom from another.

Mushroom gills

Note: It is hard to know what color your mushroom's spores will be. Since white spores will not show up on white paper, it is best to use colored paper. Choose a light color—for example, yellow or beige—in case the spores turn out to be dark.

Rocks and Fossils

Because rocks are all around us, it's easy to ignore them—at least until you get a pebble stuck in your shoe. But rocks can be a lot of fun to collect. They come in all shapes and sizes. Some are smooth and dark. Others are colorful and sparkly. Some are super hard. Others are as soft as powder. Some are as common as grains of sand. Others are rare and precious.

Unlike the animals and plants you see in the woods, rocks are not living things. But they are amazing in a different way. The plain little stone you find on the trail could be millions of years old. And, if you are very lucky, it might contain a special treat: a fossil, the telltale imprint of a plant or animal that disappeared from the earth long, long ago.

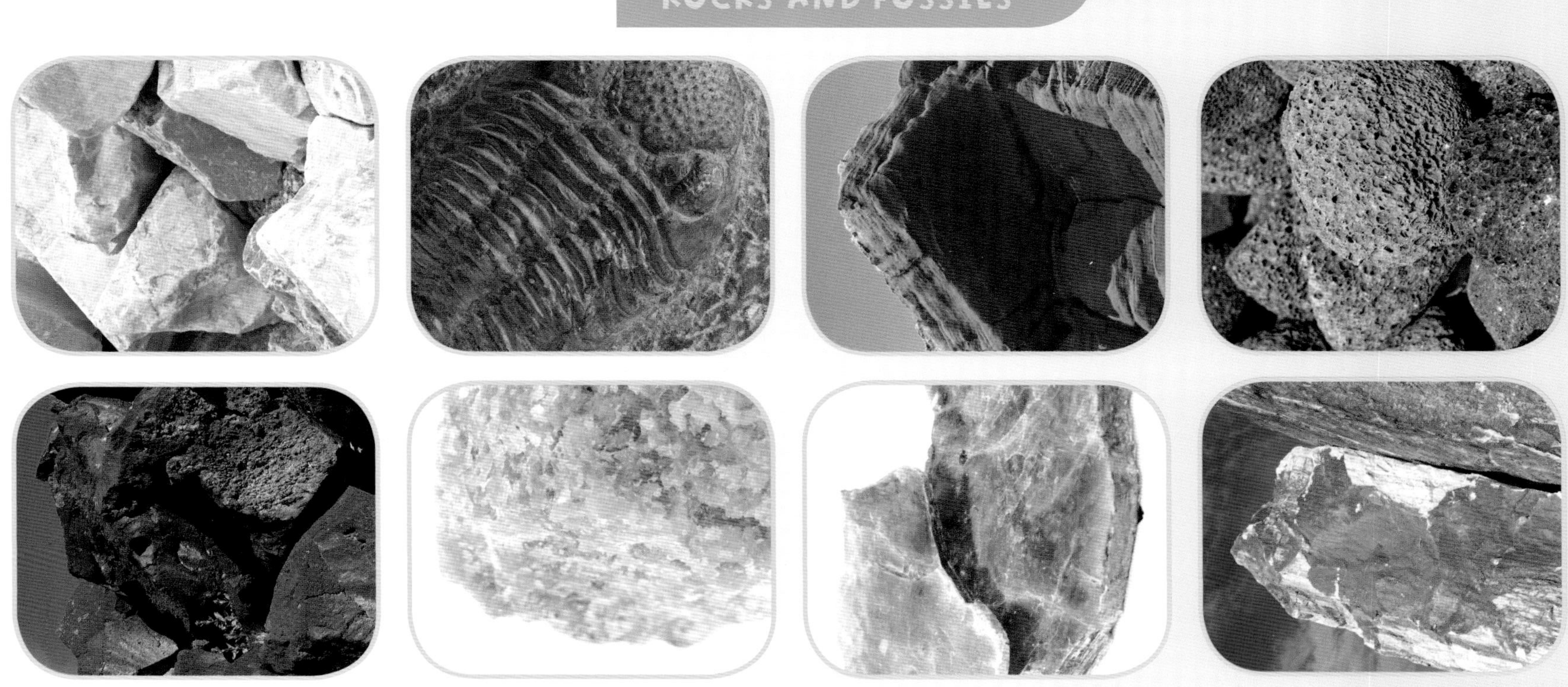

Rocks Born in Fire

Obsidian

Bubbling away beneath the earth's surface are lots of superhot melted rocks called magma. When magma makes its way to the surface, it cools and becomes solid rock. Rocks made from magma are called igneous rocks.

IGNEOUS ROCKS

Igneous rocks can be created slowly—or lightning fast. Sometimes, the melted rock is pushed up through cracks in the earth, sort of like toothpaste squeezed through a tube. It is a long, gradual trip, and the magma cools and hardens along the way. Rocks made this way are called **plutonic rocks.**

Another kind of igneous rock is created when volcanoes erupt. During an eruption, superhot magma surges up from inside the earth. Once it reaches earth's surface, magma is known as lava. Lava gushes from volcanoes (it can even shoot high into the air!) and hardens quickly. Rocks formed this way are called **volcanic rocks.**

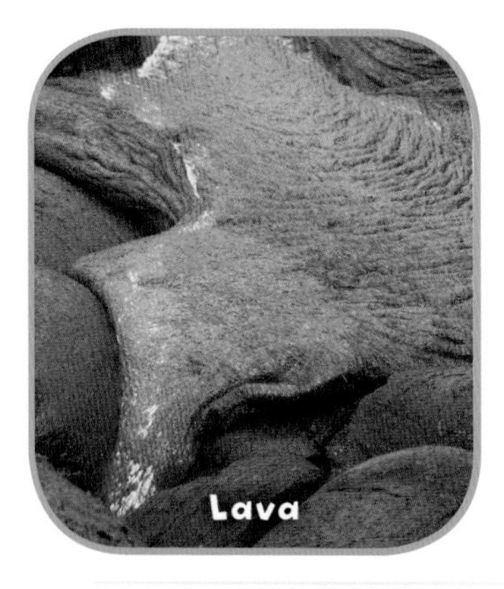
Lava

Whether the magma hardens slowly or quickly affects how it looks. Plutonic rocks are often dotted with shiny crystals that grew inside as the rock gradually cooled. Volcanic rocks are smoother.

Granite

EXAMPLES OF IGNEOUS ROCKS

Granite is the most common plutonic rock. It is usually whitish or gray. Many city buildings and street curbs are made of granite. Granite feels rough because of the mineral crystals trapped inside it. If it contains a lot of the mineral feldspar, it may be pink or red. If it contains the mineral quartz, it will sparkle.

Basalt is a volcanic rock. It is smooth and dark—gray or brown, even black. Basalt is the most common rock in the world. The ocean floor is covered in basalt.

Basalt

Another volcanic rock is **obsidian.** Obsidian is created by lava that cools so quickly it contains no crystals at all. It can be a single color or multicolored with stripes, but it is usually dark.

Pumice is volcanic rock that hardened while the lava was still filled with gas bubbles. It is extremely light—in fact, it's the only rock that floats!

Pumice

GLASSY, GLOSSY MICA

One mineral you might find inside granite is **mica.** Mica is shiny and transparent. Before glass became common, mica was used to make the windshields of early automobiles.

Mica

Layered Rocks

Some rocks are made from tiny bits of older rocks. It's all part of a humongous, super-duper, earth-wide recycling program.

Sandstone

SEDIMENTARY ROCKS

As mountains are worn down by wind and water, pieces of rock break off and are ground into ever-smaller bits. Eventually they are nothing more than grains of sand and mud called sediment. The sediment flows down rivers and into lakes and oceans. Over many, many years, these tiny grains pile up. As new layers of sand arrive, the deeper ones get pushed down. Eventually they harden into a new kind of rock called **sedimentary rock.**

You often find sedimentary rock far from the ocean. Why? Because many places in the world that are now dry were once covered with water. When you find a piece of sedimentary rock, imagine that you are standing in the middle of a long-lost ocean.

EXAMPLES OF SEDIMENTARY ROCKS

Sandstone is usually white, orange, pink, or red. When you examine sandstone, you can often see some of the individual sand grains that got stuck together hundreds of millions of years ago.

Sandstone

Limestone

Limestone is made from the shells of tiny ocean animals. These shells pile up on the ocean floor and eventually turn to rock. Limestone can be white, gray, pink, or even black. Throughout history, limestone has had many uses. The great pyramids in Egypt were built of limestone.

Limestone wall

FIELD FACT Chalk is actually a kind of limestone.

Shale is mud or clay that has turned to stone. It is usually gray, but can be black, green, or red.

Shale with fossilized leaves

CAPTURED FOREVER IN STONE!

Fossils are the outlines of plants and animals that got buried in sand and sediment long ago. The soft parts of these living things quickly rotted, but the harder parts, such as skeletons and shells, lasted much longer. Sometimes the outlines and textures of these parts were preserved in the rock, like a footprint in concrete. If you look closely at a piece of limestone or shale, you might see the impressions of shells or plants that lived hundreds of millions of years ago.

Trilobites are hard-shelled animals that lived hundreds of millions of years ago. They are extinct now, but we know about them from fossils.

Rocks of Change

Marble

When a caterpillar changes into a butterfly, we say that it has undergone metamorphosis. *Metamorphosis* means "change." A rock can go through a metamorphosis, too.

METAMORPHIC ROCKS

Incredibly hot underground magma can heat up a rock, and the pressure of being deep underground can squeeze it into a new form. When igneous or sedimentary rocks go through such big changes, they are called **metamorphic rocks.** They look and feel different from their original state and are stronger.

EXAMPLES OF METAMORPHIC ROCKS

Slate is a rock that started as shale. It is dark and smooth, and it easily splits apart into flat layers. It looks like shale but is much harder. Chalkboards are made of slate. Because slate pebbles are so flat and smooth, they make great skipping stones!

Slate

Slate can go through a second round of change, becoming an even harder kind of rock called **schist.** Schist looks very different from slate. It is bumpy. And if you look closely you can often see tiny grains inside—bits of shiny mica and garnet. Most of the island of Manhattan in New York City is made of schist. Without that solid

Schist

foundation of hard, sturdy rock, the city's skyscrapers could not have been built.

Marble is a rock that started as limestone. Marble is much harder than limestone. It can be polished and carved. Artists use it to make beautiful sculptures. Marble can be one color or many colors mixed together, like tutti-frutti ice cream. It can be white, gray, pink, or even green!

Quartzite is a rock that started as sandstone. Quartzite and sandstone look alike. To tell them apart, you have to break them! Sandstone crumbles into sand grains, but quartzite cracks into pieces.

ARROWHEADS

Arrowheads

Native Americans often shaved flint, obsidian, quartz, or other rocks to a point. They tied these sharp rocks to the ends of sticks, creating arrows or spears. Native Americans used these weapons to hunt many kinds of animals.

It has been many years since Native Americans hunted for food all over the United States, but you can still find their arrowheads. Look for them near streams and in natural caves, where Native Americans might have camped.

Animals

There are so many different kinds of animals that experts divide them into groups. Insects are animals. They have a hard outer shell, six legs, and two antennae. Beetles, butterflies, ants, and crickets are all insects. Unlike insects, birds, amphibians, reptiles, and mammals all have backbones. Birds have wings and feathers, and their young hatch from eggs.

Frogs, toads, and salamanders are amphibians. Many amphibians spend part of their lives in water and part on land. Most amphibians have thin, moist skin, and lay Jello-like eggs. Unlike amphibians, reptiles have scales on their bodies and lay eggs with leathery skins. Snakes, turtles, and lizards are reptiles. Some live in water.

People, bears, deer, bats, and raccoons are all mammals. They have hair, and most give birth to live young. In this section, you'll learn about many of the animals that make their home in the woods.

ANIMALS

Social Insects

Some insects live together in large, organized groups. Bees, wasps, and ants are called social insects because each individual devotes its efforts to the good of all.

A JOB FOR EVERY ANT

Just as police officers keep people safe, bankers handle money, and farmers grow food, each ant in a colony has a special job. Some find food. Some feed and care for the baby ants. Some are soldiers, ready to protect the nest. Insects can't talk to one another, so how do they decide who does which job? They communicate using smells.

Carpenter ant

Let's say a **carpenter ant** finds a pile of yummy potato chips that someone dropped at a picnic. One ant isn't big enough to carry all the chips back to the anthill. So the ant makes a special chemical that it leaves in its tracks. When other ants pick up this smell, they follow the first ant's path to the food and help carry it to the nest.

Formica ant

Formica ants are farmers. Just as we keep cows and drink their milk, these

ants keep "herds" of insects called aphids and eat the sweet liquid that the aphids make. **Fire ants** are reddish brown to black. They sting, so be careful!

THE BEE DANCE

Honeybees have another way to communicate. When a honeybee finds a group of flowers that are full of delicious nectar or pollen, it returns to the nest and performs a dance. The dancing bee spins in a figure-eight shape and buzzes excitedly. The speed and the movements of the dance tell the other bees how far away the flowers are and which direction they're in.

WASP ARCHITECTS

Paper wasps make beautiful homes for themselves using nothing but wood and their own spit. They scrape wood off posts and telephone poles, and collect bits of tree bark. Then they chew this stuff up and turn it into a paste from which they build large nests in trees or even on the sides of houses, beneath the roof overhang. There are many kinds of paper wasps in the United States.

Paper wasps

Flashy and Noisy Insects

Insects that light up or sing are constant reminders of the life all around us. These sounds and lights are made by male insects that are trying to attract mates.

WHAT'S THAT BLINKING?

Fireflies are a kind of beetle. (See page 60.) They have a special organ at the lower end of their bodies that makes yellow, green, or red light. Fireflies live in the eastern United States. There, as daylight turns into dusk, you will often see little lights begin to flash.

Firefly

There are different kinds of fireflies. Each one blinks in its own particular pattern so that others of its kind will recognize it. Some female fireflies take advantage of the males' eagerness to find them. They mimic the blinking pattern of a different kind of firefly. When a male of that type comes over to her, she eats him!

Fireflies are also called lightning bugs.

FIELD FACT Sometimes, lots of fireflies will flash their lights at the same time. There are places in South Carolina and Tennessee known for these spectacular firefly light shows.

WHO'S MAKING THAT SOUND?

You'll hear **cicadas** singing in the middle of the hottest summer afternoons. They are among the loudest insects.

There are many kinds of cicadas, but all are big (up to 2 inches long) with see-through wings. Cicadas have rough patches of skin on the sides of their bodies. Muscles make these patches go up and down to make a clicking sound.

Cicada

Young cicadas spend their lives underground, where they drink liquid from tree roots. In fact, some cicadas hide for 13 or 17 years before coming above ground.

There are many kinds of crickets and grasshoppers, and they make noise differently from cicadas: They rub two body parts together. **Field crickets** and **katydids** rub their two front wings. **Grasshoppers** scrape their back legs against their wings.

Field cricket

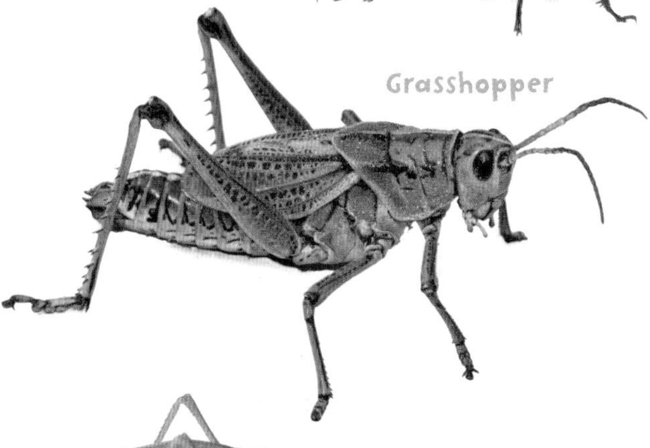

Grasshopper

Katydid

Spiders

Brown recluse

When a spider finds an animal it wants to eat, it grabs it and bites. Poison shoots out of its fangs, and the animal stops moving. Next, the spider injects a chemical that liquifies the animal's insides, so it can suck them out. Yum!

Garden spider

Spiders are not insects. They have eight legs, not six.

SPIDERS THAT WEAVE WEBS

In addition to poison, spiders make something called silk. It comes out of them like a long thread. Spider silk is very light and very strong. Some spiders use their silk to make webs.

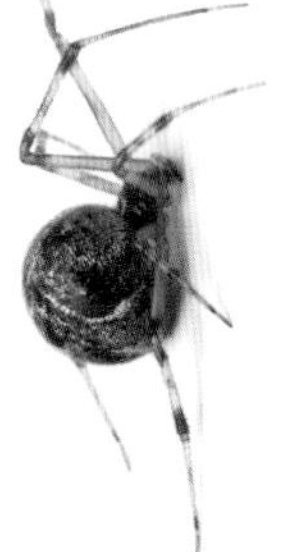

Common house spider

The **garden spider** makes a round, even web in which many lines of silk run from the center to the outer edge, like the spokes of a wheel. The **common house spider** builds a messy and tangled web, often behind open doors or on attic windows. The **black widow** also makes a disorderly web. It is one of the very few spiders in the United States whose bite can be dangerous to people. Another is the **brown recluse,** which is found in the central

Black widow

United States. If you come across a black widow or a brown recluse, avoid it and tell an adult where you spotted it.

FIELD FACT Spiders are hardly ever dangerous to people. In fact, most spiders are helpful to have around, because they eat lots of bugs that we don't like.

SPIDERS THAT HUNT

A wolf spider wraps up its meal.

Not all spiders make webs to trap their meals. **Wolf spiders** simply pounce on scurrying insects. They are fast runners and, like most other spiders, they have eight eyes, which give them excellent vision. There are many kinds of wolf spiders. The females carry their babies on their backs.

Crab spider

Crab spiders catch food by sitting and waiting, often inside a flower.

FIELD FACT Spiders can walk across ceilings or up glass windowpanes, because they have thousands and thousands of tiny hairs at the end of each of their legs that help them hold on.

Daddy longlegs

A SPIDER COUSIN

There are many kinds of **daddy longlegs,** which are also called harvestmen. They are not spiders, although they are closely related. Daddy longlegs have eight legs the way spiders do, but they have only one body segment. Spiders have two. Daddy longlegs' legs are very sensitive, helping them hear and smell what's around them.

Caterpillars

Monarch caterpillar

Caterpillars' soft bodies make perfect little meals for many insects, birds, and other animals. But caterpillars have many ways to avoid being eaten.

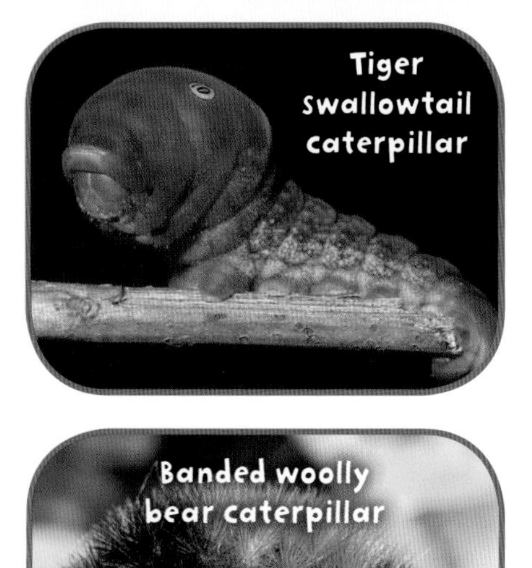

DON'T EAT ME!

Young **tiger swallowtail caterpillars** don't look like insects at all. They look more like . . . bird poop! Hungry animals often won't even notice them because they don't look like tasty food. Later, these caterpillars turn green and develop markings that look like two fake eyes to scare animals away. (See page 83.)

The **banded woolly bear caterpillar** (which will later become the Isabella tiger moth) is fuzzy. Few animals want to eat such a hairy mouthful. The **cabbage caterpillar** is green—just the right color to blend into the leaves it lives on.

The bright colors of the **monarch caterpillar** are a warning. Monarch caterpillars munch on milkweed

Cabbage caterpillar

plants. Milkweed contains poisons that build up in the caterpillars' bodies. If an animal eats a monarch caterpillar, it will feel sick.

Monarch butterfly chrysalis

SHAPE CHANGERS

Caterpillars eat and eat, mostly leaves. After a few weeks, they build a shelter for themselves called a **chrysalis** or a **cocoon.** Caterpillars that become moths make cocoons. Caterpillars that become butterflies make chrysalises. Inside these shelters, the caterpillar's body dissolves into soupy muck, and a delicate moth or butterfly takes shape.

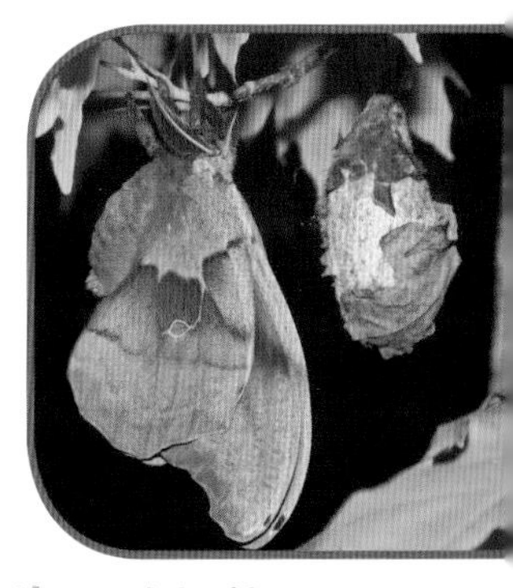

A moth next to its cocoon

MAKE IT

FRONT-ROW SEATS

Want to watch a caterpillar transform? Prop up a branch inside a terrarium. Then fill a small tub (like a clean, dry butter container) with dirt and place it inside the terrarium. Keep the terrarium in a shed or garage, where it will be exposed to outside temperatures—not in the house.

Next, go on a caterpillar hunt! When you find one, take note of what kind of plant it is on. Most caterpillars eat only one kind of plant. So you will need to add a stalk of leaves from that plant every day. Once your caterpillar builds its chrysalis or cocoon, it won't need any more care. In a couple of weeks, a butterfly or moth will come out, spread its wings, and rest until the wings dry. Then it is time to let it go!

Butterflies and Moths

Butterflies and moths start out as caterpillars. They both have thin, delicate wings that are much larger than their bodies. Both visit flowers to drink a sweet liquid called nectar.

But butterflies and moths are different in some important ways. Butterflies land with their wings folded together and pointing up. Moths land with their wings folded against their bodies or pointing out from their sides. Butterflies are active during the day. Moths are active at night.

Tiger Swallowtail

KINDS OF BUTTERFLIES

There are many types of butterflies. The swallowtails have pointy parts that stick out from their wings at the back, but their colors and patterns vary. **Tiger swallowtails** are yellow with black stripes, like a tiger. Do they look like they did as caterpillars? See pages 56 and 83 to find out.

Another butterfly family includes butterflies called whites and sulphurs. **Cabbage whites** are one of these. They were brought to the United States from Europe.

Cabbage white

The **clouded sulphur** is common all over the United States. It is an orange butterfly

Clouded sulphur

Painted lady

that lives in open fields and forest edges.

Brush-footed butterflies seem to have two pairs of legs, but if you look closely you'll see that their front pair of legs is just shorter. These butterflies use their front legs to taste their food! Some of our most beautiful butterflies, such as **mourning cloaks** and **painted ladies,** are in this family.

Mourning cloak

A SERIOUS TRAVELER

The **monarch butterfly** lives everywhere in the United States. (See what it looks like as a caterpillar on page 56.) Every fall, monarchs fly south to a few spots in Mexico and California—a trip that can be up to 3,000 miles long. There, they group together on trees and spend the winter resting. In the spring, the monarchs return home.

Monarch butterfly

MOTHS

Isabella tiger moth

The banded woolly bear caterpillar (see page 56) turns into the **Isabella tiger moth.** Like most moths, it flies at night. But a few moths, like the **hummingbird clearwing,** fly during the day. These moths hover in one place as they sip nectar from flowers, the way hummingbirds do.

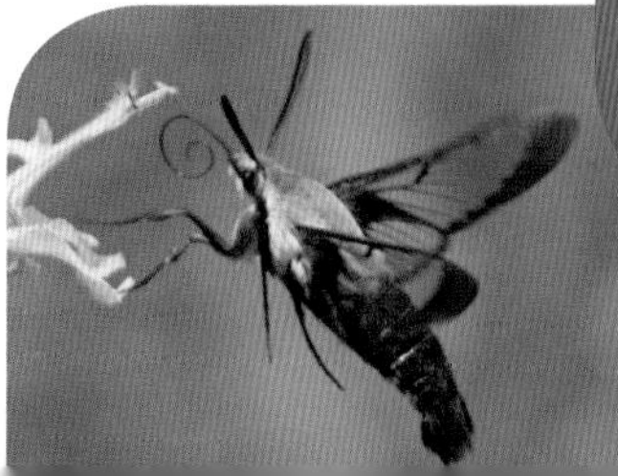
Hummingbird clearwing

Beetles

Soldier beetle

Beetles come in many shapes and colors. Some beetles are long and thin. Others are round or oval. Some are shiny green or gold. Others are the color of wood or sand.

Stag beetle

One group of beetles, **stag beetles,** looks like tiny bulls because they have horns sticking out of their heads. **Fireflies** are another kind of beetle. (see page 52.)

FIELD FACT About one-quarter of all the animals in the world are beetles! Many thousands of beetles live in the United States.

WELCOME AND UNWELCOME GUESTS

Different types of beetles have different habits and diets that affect how humans react to them. There are many kinds of **ladybird beetles** in the United States. You probably know them as ladybugs. People often say that ladybugs bring good luck. Whether or not that is true, almost all ladybugs eat insects that destroy crops and garden plants. So people are happy to see them.

Round-shaped ladybug

Every kind of ladybug has a different number of spots. One of the most common ladybugs in the United States is the **round-shaped ladybug.** Also known as the seven-spotted ladybug, it has (you guessed it!) seven spots.

Soldier beetles are also welcome visitors. They, too, eat insects that harm crops and plants. There are many kinds of soldier beetles.

Weevils are beetles with mouthparts that look like long noses. **Acorn weevils** use their mouthparts to drill through the hard shells of acorns to eat the nuts inside. Other weevils eat crops and garden plants. They are pests.

Acorn weevil

HISSING AND CLICKING

Junebugs are wide beetles that can grow to be longer than your pinky finger. They are clumsy flyers and often bang against window screens at night because they are attracted to the lights inside. The **ten-lined june beetle,** which lives in the western United States, makes a hissing sound when scared. **Click beetles** bounce into the air by curving their bodies, then snapping themselves straight. They make a loud clicking sound as they do this.

Junebug

Ten-lined june beetle

Click beetle

Flying insects can be fun to watch as they zip around doing their "bzzz-ness."

Black fly

BLACK FLIES—OUCH!

Black flies are small, but their bites pack a big punch! Some people call black flies "buffalo gnats" because their bodies are hunched like the shoulders of a bison. Black flies may annoy humans, but they are a sign of a healthy forest. When streams are dirty, black fly eggs do not hatch.

MOSQUITOES

Many kinds of mosquitoes live in the United States, but only the females bite humans. Male mosquitoes never bother people. They eat nectar from flowers. But the females need blood to grow their eggs.

Mosquitoes can be a big problem because they can spread disease. Yet mosquitoes are an important part of the forest world. Many animals, including frogs, bats, and birds, depend on them for food.

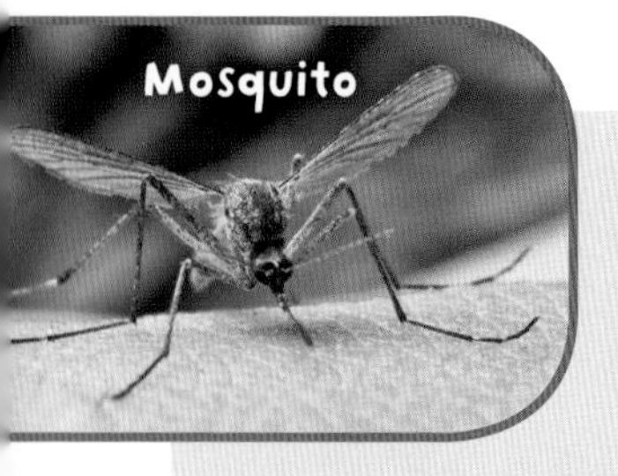
Mosquito

MOSQUITO MOUTHPARTS

The mouthparts of the female mosquito looks like a built-in straw. To feed, the mosquito sticks this straw, called a proboscis, into a person's skin. It then injects saliva into the wound. The saliva thins your blood so the mosquito can drink it more easily. It's the mosquito's spit that makes the bites itch!

DRAGONFLIES AND DAMSELFLIES

Blue-eyed darner dragonfly

By the edge of a pond you may see **dragonflies** and **damselflies** flitting by. With two pairs of wings, these critters are expert flyers. They reach speeds of 60 miles per hour, and they can hover in the air like helicopters. They are hunters, grabbing mosquitoes and other insects from the air. They are harmless to humans.

Damselflies and dragonflies are easy to tell apart. Damselflies have thinner bodies. And when it isn't flying, the damselfly keeps its wings pressed along its body. The dragonfly sticks its wings straight out.

Northern blue damselfly

DRAGONFLY VS. DAMSELFLY

Here are two of the most common types of dragonflies and damselflies in the United States. Can you tell which is a dragonfly and which is a damselfly?

Common whitetail

American rubyspot

Animal Recyclers

Some of the smallest animals have the biggest jobs. They are members of nature's cleanup crew. That means they eat dead plants and animals. It may sound gross, but it is important work. Imagine if dead things just kept piling up!

Creatures that eat dead things are called decomposers. As they chow down, they release useful chemicals. These chemicals help new living things grow.

Pill bug

WHO LIVES UNDER THAT ROCK?

Turn over a stone or old log. Chances are you will see plenty of **pill bugs.** (Some people call them roly-polies.) Pill bugs feed on dead wood, turning mighty trees into dirt. They look like fossils. When they get scared, they protect themselves by rolling into a ball.

Another creature you might find under a log is a **millipede.** The name means "thousand feet," but even the longest millipede has only 376 or so. It's easy to confuse the millipede with the **centipede** ("hundred feet"), but they are different.

Millipede

Garden centipede

A millipede has two sets of legs per body segment; centipedes have one set. Millipedes are mild mannered. They eat broken-down bits of plants. Centipedes are not decomposers. They hunt and eat insects. Centipedes bite, so take care.

PARTNERS IN SLIME

Earthworm

Earthworms move through dirt, swallowing it by the mouthful. They digest some of it and poop out the rest. If you look on the ground in the forest or even your own backyard, you might see delicate coils of dirt. These are called castings. They are the undigested dirt that passed through an earthworm's body. Castings are full of healthy nutrients.

Slugs are another kind of decomposer. They are a lot like snails without shells. Slugs are covered in mucus—the same stuff our snot is made of! Mucus helps slugs slide along the ground. Bright yellow **banana slugs** are often found on the floors of redwood forests. The **giant garden slug** is common in many states.

Banana slug

The giant garden slug, or leopard slug, can grow up to 8 inches long.

FEATURE

Good Smells, Bad Smells

Nature is full of smells, but our noses are not sensitive enough to notice them all. We do not smell the chemicals that ants make to tell one another where to find food. Nor can we tell which of our neighbors' pets have visited our yard just by sniffing the ground, the way a dog can. But we still smell plenty of things—some yucky, some pleasant.

TAKE THIS AS A WARNING

Some animals make bad smells to keep their enemies away. **Skunks** spray a stinky liquid when they are threatened. After wearing that disgusting "perfume" for a few days, an animal will think twice before bothering a skunk again. **Stinkbugs** also make a bad-smelling liquid to protect themselves from being eaten.

Stink bug

Animals are not the only ones. Some plants use smells to defend themselves, too. Pinch the leaves of a cedar or eucalyptus tree and sniff. Many evergreen trees have strong smells. So do the plants that we use to flavor our food, such as **basil, sage,** and **mint.** These odors keep away insects that would otherwise eat the plants' leaves. But people aren't insects. We like these smells.

Basil

Sage

Mint

FIELD FACT Skunks usually give a few warnings before they spray. They will stomp or hiss before lifting their tail and unleashing their stinky weapon.

COME TO ME!

Skunk cabbage

Some plants make stinky smells not to drive animals away but to attract them! For example, **skunk cabbage** needs flies in order to make seeds. Flies like to lay their eggs in rotting things, so just imagine what skunk cabbage smells like! Just as eucalyptus smells yucky to insects but nice to us, skunk cabbage smells heavenly to flies—but to us, more like poop.

Roses, magnolias, and many other flowers attract flying insects with odors that we like, too. Bees and butterflies like to visit sweet-smelling flowers, and their visits help the flowers make seeds.

Magnolia

Rose

Songbirds

When you are in the woods, take time to be perfectly quiet. Look for quick movements. And listen. Male birds are often the most colorful, and sing the loudest. They are trying to impress female birds, not us.

American robin

Spotted towhee

House wren

FROM BOTTOM TO TOP

Start by scanning the ground. There, especially in clearings or parks, you are likely to see the **American robin,** with its dark gray head and rust-colored chest. This bird hops a few steps, then stops, cocks its head to one side, and looks for an earthworm to grab. A **towhee** has similar coloring to a robin, except a towhee's chest is white with reddish patches on each side. Towhees rustle in the underbrush rather than strut in the open.

The **house wren** darts around on low branches with its tail held high, snatching insects from the leaves.

Songbirds can be show-offs. Some will sit at the top of a tree or the tip of a branch, belting out their melodies. **Song sparrows** are small brownish birds. They don't look like much, but they have a long, beautiful song. And boy, is it loud! **Yellow warblers** are dainty, lemon-colored birds. Their song is short and simple, and they sing it over and over. The **northern mockingbird** copies the songs of other birds.

Song Sparrow

Northern mockingbird

FIELD FACT Mockingbirds are amazing mimics. Some have even learned to sound like car alarms.

I KNOW THAT SONG!

Yellow warbler

Often the best way to "spot" a bird is with your ears, not your eyes. Birds can hide in the leaves of trees, but they can't keep you from hearing them sing.

Every kind of bird makes its own special sounds. The yellow warbler has a high-pitched monotone that sounds like "sweet, sweet, sweet, I'm-so-sweet." The robin seems to say: "cheerily, cheer up, cheer up, cheerily, cheer up." The towhee has a three-syllable call—two short notes and a long trill—that sounds like "Drink-your-tea!"

Once you learn to recognize a few bird calls, you will feel like the forest is full of old friends. Learn them by listening to recordings at www.allaboutbirds.org.

Songbirds in Winter

It can be easier to see birds in the winter because many trees have lost their leaves. Even though a lot of birds fly south for the winter, some stay put. Others arrive from places farther north.

Male northern cardinal

You may catch sight of a **northern cardinal** against a snowy white branch. Female cardinals are brownish, but the males are bright red. Both have pointy feathers on their heads called crests and black markings around their beaks.

Female northern cardinal

American goldfinches are bright yellow with black wings. They make a high-pitched, monotone call that has the same rhythm as a person saying, "po-TA-to chip, po-TA-to chip." Another kind of finch, the **house finch,** is a larger, drabber bird. But male house finches have reddish heads and chests and a cheerful, twittery song.

American goldfinch

Male house finches

Titmouse

Chickadee

Two of the most common winter birds are tiny, lively, and curious. **Chickadees** have black caps and bibs under their chins. **Titmice** are mostly gray with tiny tufts of feathers on top of their heads. Chickadees and titmice are natural acrobats. They can even catch insects in their beaks while hanging upside down.

White-breasted nuthatches are grayish blue on their backs and white on their cheeks and bellies. The males have black caps. Nuthatches eat beetles and other insects living inside tree bark. You may see them on tree trunks, working their way down a tree, headfirst. They also like seeds and nuts.

Male white-breasted nuthatch

FOCUS ON FEATHERS

Birds regularly shed feathers and grow new ones. Some feathers are fluffy. They grow close to the bird's skin to keep it warm. These are called body feathers. Other feathers help birds fly. These flight feathers have a central spine called a shaft and many thin branches called barbs sticking out on either side. Cut a feather in half. Why do you think the shaft is hollow? That's right: The less a bird weighs, the more easily it can get off the ground.

Jays, Crows, and Ravens

Unlike some smaller songbirds, which can be relatively shy, these birds hop and flit about in the open. They spend a lot of time in groups. Sometimes, they work together to find food. You may see them "arguing," or playing a game that looks like follow-the-leader.

Blue jay

Steller's jay

The **blue jay** is a large bird that catches the eye with its bright blue back and tail feathers, black face markings, and the pointy crest on its head. The blue jay lives in the eastern and central United States. In the western part of the country, you'll find the **Steller's jay,** a darker bird that also has a head crest. Both kinds of jays are bossy, noisy birds that will steal your picnic lunch if you give them half a chance.

FIELD FACT Steller's jays can mimic the sounds of other birds, as well as cats, dogs, chickens, and squirrels. They can even make noises that resemble the sounds of electronics or mechanical objects.

The **black-billed magpie** is another large and striking bird. It is black and white, with a very long black tail. Magpies live in the western United States.

Black-billed magpie

The **American crow** is all black. It makes a loud, harsh caw sound that you have probably heard many times, even if you never realized what it was. Crows flock together, often in big groups. The **common raven** is a large all-black bird. Native Americans have many stories about the raven's sneaky ways. Ravens are larger than crows, with a bigger bill and a longer tail. Ravens make a deep croak, instead of a caw.

Common raven

BIRD BRAINS

Jays, crows, magpies, and ravens are all extremely intelligent. For instance, they use twigs and blades of grass as tools to help them find food. Crows have even been known to drop hard-to-crack nuts on the street, wait for a car to run them over, then return to pick up the edible parts.

American crow

Woodpeckers

If you see a bird with a thick head and straight back pecking patiently at a tree trunk, it's probably a woodpecker. Woodpeckers use their beaks to drill into bark, then they grab insects with their sticky tongues. Some woodpeckers drink the tree's sap—the sweet liquid that farmers turn into maple syrup.

Even when you don't see or hear a woodpecker, your detective skills may tell you that one has been there. Look carefully at the holes in trees to figure out whether they were made by a woodpecker.

Pileated woodpecker

The **pileated woodpecker** is huge. It has pointy red feathers on top of its head, a black body, and black and white stripes on its cheeks and neck. It makes round or oval holes the size of a grown-up's fist.

Male downy woodpecker

The **downy woodpecker** is the smallest woodpecker in the United States. Some of its feathers are black and white like a checkerboard. Males have a bright red spot on the back of the head.

You can tell when a **sapsucker** has been on a tree because of the lines of small holes it makes. It almost looks as if the bird used a ruler!

Sapsucker

The **northern flicker** is a large brownish-gray bird with a dark collar, polka dots on its chest, and dark markings on its back. When it flies you'll see it has a white rump and either golden yellow or pinkish red under its wings. The flicker has odd habits for a woodpecker. It spends most of its time on the ground, eating ants.

Northern flicker

FIELD FACT How do woodpeckers walk up a tree trunk or perch on it without falling off? A woodpecker's foot has two toes that face forward and two that face backward. This helps them balance. Their strong tails also prop them up.

SPOTTING WOODPECKERS

Instead of singing to let other birds know where they are, woodpeckers do something called drumming. They pound their bills on the loudest thing they can find. This could be a tree or even the aluminum siding on someone's house. You can learn to recognize the sound of woodpeckers drumming at www.allaboutbirds.org.

Hummingbirds

Like living helicopters, hummingbirds hover in one place by beating their wings incredibly fast: up to 200 times per second!

Male ruby-throated hummingbird

TINY AND COLORFUL

Hummingbirds are small, about the size of your hand. And they weigh even less than you might think—just a fraction of an ounce. Hummingbirds feed on insects and on the nectar found inside flowers. The feathers on hummingbirds' heads are bright and shiny.

Female black-chinned hummingbird

The **ruby-throated hummingbird** is the only hummingbird that lives in the eastern and central United States. It buzzes by so quickly that you may only see a flash of green (on the back and top of its head) and red (under the chin of the males).

Anna's hummingbird, the **black-chinned hummingbird,** and the **rufous hummingbird** are some of the hummingbirds in the western United States. Anna's hummingbird has similar colors to the ruby-throated hummingbird except that it has red on top of its head. Male black-chinned hummingbirds have a black

Male Anna's hummingbird

throat with a thin purple band around it. Females have some green on their backs and gray underneath. The male rufous hummingbird is bright orange. Female rufous hummingbirds are green on their backs with an orange spot at the throat.

Male rufous hummingbird

FIELD FACT Hummingbirds can fly up, down, sideways, backward, and upside down!

TINY TRAVELERS

Like many birds, hummingbirds migrate. In the fall, they fly south to spend the winter in places where food is easier to find. In the spring, they return—often going to the exact same tree where they nested the year before. Some fly for more than 12 hours without stopping. Scientists are amazed that such tiny birds have so much strength.

BRING HUMMINGBIRDS TO YOU

One great way to observe hummingbirds is to grow the plants that attract them, such as bee balm, cardinal flower, honeysuckle, and trumpet vine. Or you can hang a hummingbird feeder. Fill it with sugar water, and the birds will come. Be sure to place the feeder where hummingbirds will be safe from cats or other animals that might hurt them.

Hummingbirds visit only brightly colored flowers, especially red ones.

Birds of Prey

Hawks and eagles are called birds of prey. They have amazing eyesight, fly incredibly fast, and are skilled hunters. They also have sharp claws called talons. The word *prey* refers to the animals that these birds eat. Other birds in this group, such as vultures, feed on dead animals.

Red-tailed hawks can even catch birds in flight.

HAWKS

Hawks' eyes are so powerful they can see great distances. It is as if they have built-in binoculars. A **red-tailed hawk** can spot a rabbit or a mouse from its perch high in a tree. Then it can swoop down at speeds of up to 50 miles per hour to grab it.

Red-tailed hawks are large with thick, rounded wings and wide tails. You can tell them from other hawks because of the reddish color of their tail feathers. You are most likely to see red-tails on the sides of roads or in clearings.

The largest hawk in the United States is the **bald eagle.**

Bald eagles are huge. Their wingspan can be more than 7 feet wide!

VULTURES

Unlike hawks, vultures do not kill their own food. They eat animals that are already dead. **Turkey vultures** often fly over highways, looking for animals that have been hit by cars. They also scan the edges of rivers to spot fish that have washed ashore. Turkey vultures are bald. Having no feathers on their heads makes it easier to stay clean when chowing on messy dead animals.

Turkey vulture

HAWK OR VULTURE?

There are two ways to tell a turkey vulture from a hawk in flight. Seen from the front, the turkey vulture's wings make a V shape. Hawks make more of a straight line. During flight, the turkey vulture tilts itself to one side and then the other in a motion similar to a person trying to keep his or her balance while walking a tightrope. Hawks, on the other hand, fly straight.

Turkey vulture in flight

Owls

Owls are hunters like hawks and eagles. But unlike hawks, which are active during the day, owls are active at night. Owls have large eyes that see very well and help them hunt in the dark. They also have an amazing sense of hearing.

Owls can hear the slightest movement of an animal among leaves and branches. More than that, an owl can tell which of its ears heard the sound first. The owl then turns its head until the sound reaches both ears at the same time. Then the owl knows that the animal is straight ahead.

FIELD FACT Owls have twice as many neck bones as people do. That means they can turn their heads all the way around to look behind their backs!

The **great horned owl** is enormous—up to 2 feet tall. It does not really have horns, though. The spikes you see on its head are just tufts of feathers.

Screech owls are small owls that also have tufts of feathers on top of their heads. They

Great horned owl

catch flying insects, as well as mice and small birds.

Barn owls have bright white undersides. Their heart-shaped faces are unusual and hard to forget. These owls often nest in barns or other buildings. Some people who have seen the silent white flash of a barn owl flying by in the night believe they've spotted a ghost.

Owl pellet

NATURE FINDS

OWL PELLETS

Owls eat all kinds of animals: mice, rabbits, snakes, birds, and even other owls. They swallow their food whole. But owls cannot digest the fur, bones, teeth, and feathers of the animals they eat. These parts get packed into a small bundle called a pellet. A few hours later, the owl throws up, and a pellet drops out.

The best place to look for owl pellets is under a tree where an owl hangs out. Groups of smaller birds often try to drive owls away. So if you ever notice a bunch of crows, jays, or other birds making a lot of noise and flying around a tree, there may be an owl in the tree.

If you find an owl pellet, use a toothpick or tweezers to carefully open it up. See if you can find a tiny skull and bones inside.

Hiding in Plain Sight

Have you ever wanted to be invisible? Some animals do, too. If they can't be seen, they won't get eaten. When an animal blends into its surroundings, it is using camouflage.

Boreal owl

An animal's color can help it avoid its enemies. This **boreal owl,** found in the western United States, has the same gray-and-white pattern as the balsam fir tree it lives in.

Other animals can change their coloring to match their surroundings. When the **gray tree frog** rests on a leaf, the frog turns green. When it climbs a branch, it turns gray again. That way, it's always hard to spot.

Gray tree frog on green leaves

Gray tree frog on tree bark

For a few animals, camouflage is a way of life. These critters look like dead leaves, thorns, or branches—anything but a yummy snack. For example, can you tell that the "twig" below has legs? It's a **stick bug**! Different kinds of stick bugs can be found all over the United States.

Tiger swallowtail caterpillar

Fake eyes

The real eyes are here.

STAYING SAFE BY STANDING OUT

Sometimes, animals protect themselves by standing out rather than blending in. Their trick is to seem bigger or scarier than they really are. For example, the **tiger swallowtail caterpillar** has big fake "eyes" on its head. These markings seem to say, "Watch out! I'm big, and I will bite you back." If you were a hungry bird, what would you do?

Birds People Eat

We appreciate birds for their beauty and their songs. But some birds are tasty, too. Just think: What would Thanksgiving be without a turkey?

POULTRY IN THE WILD

The chickens you eat are raised on farms. Years ago, before supermarkets, wild birds were an important source of food for people. And it is still legal to hunt some birds in many parts of the United States.

The **wild turkey** is a very large, fat bird. It is dark colored and has a fan-shaped tail. Turkeys have no feathers on their heads.

Male turkeys have weird-looking red fleshy parts called wattles on their necks.

Turkeys are powerful flyers, but they tend to walk a lot too, looking for acorns, fruits, insects, and other good things to eat. They hang out in groups. On your hikes, you may run into a mother turkey with her youngsters or several families traveling together. Because they are so big and they move in groups, you won't have to search for wild turkeys. You'll hear them coming!

Years ago, wild turkeys were hunted so much that not many were left. But people worked hard to help them, and now they are common in many parts of the country.

Mourning doves are plump brown or gray birds with delicate heads and black eyes. The word *mourning* means sad. The doves got their name because of their song, which is a sad-sounding, five-note melody. The dove remains common throughout the United States—even though hunters kill and eat more than 20 million mourning doves every year.

Mourning dove

The **wood duck** is so colorful, it almost looks unreal. Wood ducks spend a lot of time on lakes and rivers. But unlike most other ducks, they nest in holes in trees. It's quite a thrill to see a bunch of newly hatched wood ducks jump down from a tree and make their way to water. Wood ducks are hunted for their meat and their feathers.

FIELD FACT Fly fisherman use wood duck feathers to lure trout. To the fish, the shimmery feathers look like a tasty insect.

Wood duck

Bats

Bats fly, but they are not birds. They are mammals. Instead of laying eggs, they grow their babies inside their bodies, the way people do.

These strange-looking creatures are nocturnal, which means they come out only at night. Many people are scared of them. But bats are not dangerous. In fact, bats are helpful. They eat mosquitoes and other insects people don't like—a lot of them. A bat can eat half its body weight in insects in one night. That's like you eating 40 hamburgers in a single day!

Big brown bat

Common in North America, the **little brown bat** is well named. Its body is usually only 2 to 4 inches long. The **big brown bat** has a body that is more like 4 to 5 inches long.

Little brown bat

GETTING AROUND IN THE DARK

Bats fly at night. But they don't rely on their eyes to get around. They have a special ability called echolocation. As bats fly, they make sounds—noises so high pitched we can't hear them. These sounds hit trees, walls, and everything they reach and bounce back to the bats' ears. A bat can tell, from how the sounds have changed, exactly what is around it.

FIELD FACT Many bats live in caves. The cave floors are covered in something that looks like dirt but isn't. It's bat poop, known as guano.

GROUP LIVING

Many bats live in large groups. Thousands of **Mexican free-tailed bats** live under a bridge in the city of Austin, Texas. Huge crowds gather to watch them come out at sunset.

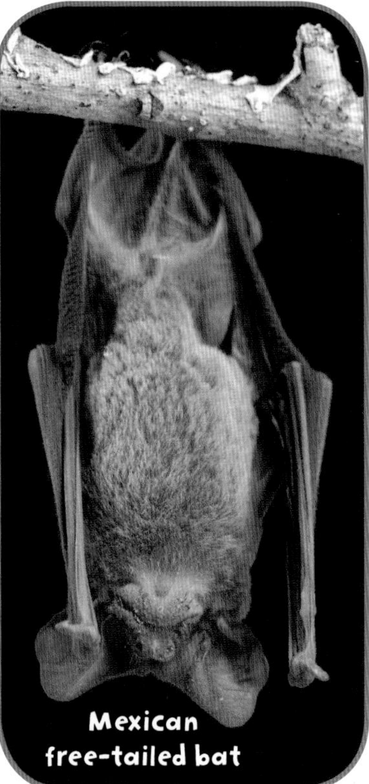
Mexican free-tailed bat

FIELD FACT You've heard of the vampire bat, right? Well, don't worry. Out of nearly 1,000 types of bats, only three suck animals' blood.

MAKE IT

HELP KEEP BATS SAFE

Bats need a place to rest during the day. They do this on trees, in caves, in barns, and even behind the shutters of people's houses. Put up a bat box to help bats find a home. The bats will reward you by eating your mosquitoes. You can even build your own bat box. With a grown-up, do an online search for "making your own bat box" to find information and building instructions.

Bat box

Frogs

You'll often see frogs sitting quietly in water with just their eyes and nose showing. But frogs also live on the ground, underground, and even in trees. Frogs breathe the way we do, using their lungs. But they also breathe through their skin.

FIELD FACT It's fun to pick up frogs, but it's not good for them. Their skin is so sensitive that the sunscreen, bug spray, or even leftover soap on your hands can hurt them.

The **American bullfrog** is the largest frog in the United States. Its body can measure up to 8 inches, and that's not including its legs. Bullfrogs will eat anything they can swallow: dragonflies, fish, snakes, turtles, and even other frogs. Bullfrogs puff out their throats like a balloon to make loud, deep croaks. They can be found in most parts of the United States.

American bullfrog

The **leopard frog** lives in ponds and streams all over the United States. You will often find them in the grass. Leopard frogs leave the water to find spiders and insects to eat.

Leopard frog

The **wood frog** lives in Alaska, most of Canada, and the northeastern United States. During the winter, it does something amazing. It freezes like a popsicle! Pieces of ice form inside its body. Its heart stops beating. It stops breathing. When wood frogs warm up again, they are as good as new. The frog has special antifreeze chemicals that make sure that ice forms only in parts of the body where it does no harm.

Wood frog

FROG SONGS

In the spring, male frogs often sing loudly at night. Singing is how they attract female frogs. The **Pacific chorus frog,** which lives in the western United States, makes the well-known "ribbit" sound. In the eastern United States, the **spring peeper** makes a high-pitched peep. Groups of spring peepers sound like a wonderful chorus of sleigh bells.

Spring peeper

Pacific chorus frog

Toads

Toads are a kind of frog. Both are amphibians. The word *amphibian* means "two lives," because the animals live both in water and on land.

WHAT MAKES A TOAD A TOAD?

Toads don't have wet, slippery skin. A toad's skin is dry and bumpy. Other frogs tend to spend more time in water, while toads spend more time on land.

LIFE CYCLE

Tadpole

All frogs, including toads, lay their eggs in water. Usually, the eggs turn into tadpoles—fishy-looking swimmers with long tails. After the tadpole stage, the legs grow, the tail shrinks, and the creature begins to look like the hopping critter you see on land. Spend time at the edge of a pond and you may see toad or frog eggs.

Most frogs lay their eggs in blobs, like bunches of grapes.

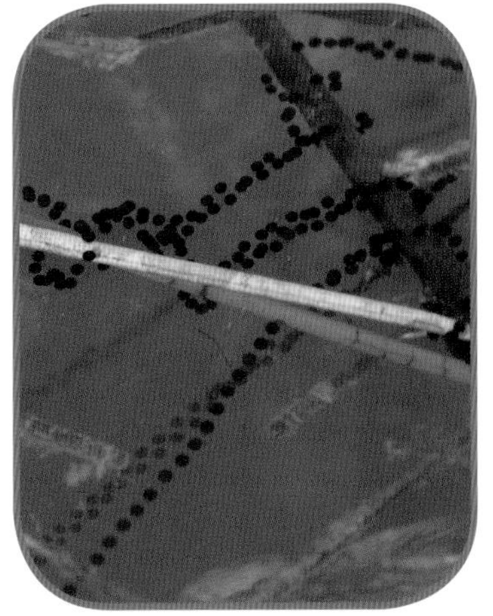

Toad eggs are like strings of black beads held together by clear jelly.

American toad

BURROWING TOADS

In the fall, the **American toad** digs a hole in the ground with its strong back legs. There it stays, barely moving, until winter is over. The American toad lives in the eastern United States.

Woodhouse's toad

Woodhouse's toads also bury themselves. The first warm rain of spring wakes them, and they come to the surface. Sometimes on a spring night after it rains, the ground is covered with hopping toads. It almost seems like they appeared by magic.

FIELD FACT Toads blink when they swallow.

Western toad

TOXIC TOADS!

Many animals have ways to avoid being eaten. Some toads puff up so that they are difficult to swallow. Others, like the **western toad,** have chemical defenses. The large bumps behind a western toad's eyes and the smaller ones on its skin make special poisons. Any animal that tries to eat this type of toad will feel like its mouth is on fire and will spit out the toad. An animal that swallows a western toad will feel sick and will probably never eat one again. Scientists are trying to turn the chemicals toads make into medicine.

Salamanders

Like frogs and toads, salamanders are amphibians. They are born in water, but spend much of their lives on land. Each spring, salamanders return to where they were born.

COLORFUL CRITTERS

Some salamanders completely change their looks as they age. For example, after living on land for about two years, the **red eft** turns green and becomes the **red-spotted newt.** Found in the eastern United States, the red-spotted newt lives in streams, marshes, or ponds.

Red eft

Red-spotted newt

Soon after a **tiger salamander** is grown, it leaves its pond for the forest. There, it lives under rotten logs or rocks and in other cool, dark places. It eats worms, crickets, and even mice. Although the tiger salamander is large (usually 6 to 8 inches long) with gold splotches, it can be hard to find because it comes out mostly at night.

Tiger salamanders can live to be 20 or 30 years old.

The same is true for the **spotted salamander.** Tiger salamanders live in the eastern and western United States. Spotted salamanders live in the eastern United States.

Spotted Salamander

FIELD FACT Salamanders' back legs grow more slowly than their front legs. That's the opposite of frogs and toads, whose back legs develop earlier.

MARCH OF THE SALAMANDERS

On the first warm, rainy nights of spring, many salamanders travel from the woods to ponds and puddles to mate and lay eggs. On these evenings, thousands of salamanders are on the move. Sometimes they must cross roads, and they get squashed. In some places, people have built tunnels under roads to help salamanders travel safely.

Here are a few tips for salamander spotting in the dark.

- Ask your parents if they will go with you to see the march of the salamanders.
- Call a local nature center and ask about the best places to see the salamanders.
- Wear boots and a poncho.
- Bring a flashlight—and a camera!

MISSING A LEG? NO PROBLEM.

If an animal bites off a salamander's tail or leg, that missing limb will grow back again. Imagine if humans could grow back a finger or even a hand that got cut off! That's exactly what scientists hope to learn to do, by studying the salamander's amazing ability.

Snakes

Water moccasin

POISONOUS

How do snakes move so well without arms or legs? Special scales on their bellies grip the ground, while their muscles push their bodies forward bit by bit.

Many snakes are shy and calm. Even the poisonous ones don't attack unless someone bothers them or steps on them by mistake.

HOW SNAKES EAT

Garter Snake

A snake's jaws can open wide enough for a meal that is larger than the snake's own head. A harmless snake found around the United States is the **garter snake,** which has long stripes down the length of its body. Garter snakes grab and stun a mouse or small bird, then swallow it. Other harmless snakes, such as the **kingsnake,** squeeze an animal to death before eating it.

Snakes take at least a couple of days to digest a big lump of food. They might not eat again for a while.

POISONOUS SNAKES

It's important to recognize dangerous snakes.

POISONOUS

Rattlesnake

POISONOUS

Rattlesnakes, which can be found across the United States, make a warning sound by shaking the hard scales at the tips of their tails. **Copperheads** and **water moccasins** are two other poisonous snakes. They live in the central and eastern United States.

Copperhead

The **coral snake,** found in the southern and southwestern United States, has colorful red, yellow, and black bands. Some harmless snakes, such as the **milk snake,** look like the coral snake, but their pattern is different. Can you tell what this rhyme means? "Red then yellow kills a fellow. Red then black, friend of Jack."

Milk Snake

FIELD FACT Snakes are cool and dry. Their smooth scales are made of the same material as our fingernails!

Coral Snake

POISONOUS

NATURE FINDS

SUPER SHEDDERS

Snakes grow all their lives, but their skin doesn't grow with them. So once in a while, a snake rubs its head on a rock to split open its top layer of skin. Then it wriggles out of it. Look for delicate snake skins on your walks.

Snake skin

Turtles

Standing at the edge of a pond, you'll notice rocks and logs. But wait! Look closely. Do you see little lumps on the rocks? They may be turtles.

Painted turtle

TURTLES IN THE SUN

On sunny days, **painted turtles** come out of the water to warm themselves. They'll stay in one place for hours without moving. Painted turtles have red, orange, and yellow stripes on their faces and bodies. They live all over the United States.

Another turtle you are likely to see sunning itself is the **red-eared slider.** This turtle is named for the red slashes on each side of its head, and for its habit of sliding quickly off rocks and back into the water when it gets nervous. These turtles live in the southern United States, California, and northwestern states.

Red-eared slider

PROTECTIVE SHELLS

A turtle's hard shell is made of bone covered by tiles called scutes. Scutes are made of keratin, the same material that human fingernails and snake scales are made of. The bone underneath is attached to the animal's ribs and spine. Because the shell is part of the turtle's skeleton, the animal can feel pain and pressure through it.

Many turtles can pull their heads and legs inside their shells to protect themselves. Some, like the **box turtle,** can even "lock" themselves in by closing all the openings. Box turtles have unique yellow patterns on their shells. They live in the eastern and central United States.

FIELD FACT Only land turtles can pull their heads and legs inside their shells. Sea turtles cannot.

WATCH YOUR FINGERS!

Another common turtle is the **snapping turtle,** which lives in most of the United States. This turtle has strong jaws that snap shut on plants, insects, ducks, and other water birds. If you ever see one on land, keep your distance because it might bite. In the water, though, snappers tend to avoid people.

Snapping turtles keep growing their entire lives. The oldest ones can weigh as much as 75 pounds!

Lizards and Alligators

Like snakes and turtles, lizards are reptiles. Reptiles are cold-blooded. That means that their body temperature changes with the weather. Lizards sun themselves when they want to warm up. Look for them sitting very still in rocky areas or forest clearings.

COMMON LIZARDS

Fence lizards often sunbathe on top of fence posts. They live in California and much of the rest of the United States. The ones in California are often called blue bellies because—you guessed it!—they have bright blue bellies. **Alligator lizards** are also common in the western United States.

Green anoles live in trees. Anoles can change color. They are bright green when they are healthy and calm. When sick or upset, they turn brown. The males have loose red skin under their necks that they puff up when they want to show off. Green anoles live in the southeastern United States.

TAKE MY TAIL, PLEASE

Many lizards have an unusual way of protecting themselves. If an animal grabs them by the tail, they throw it off like a piece of unwanted clothing—without even bleeding! The blue tail of the **western skink** keeps wriggling after it falls off, as if it were alive. These movements fool other animals into following the tail rather than the lizard. Later, the skink will grow a new tail. The western skink is found in the western and southwestern United States.

Alligator

CHOMP, CHOMP!

Alligators look like giant lizards, but they belong to a different part of the reptile family tree. They live in swampy areas, rivers, streams, lakes, and ponds in the southeastern United States.

Alligators hatch from eggs on land. They are born small, about 8 inches long. But over the next few years they can grow to be 10 feet long or even longer. Alligators have long snouts lined with sharp teeth. Their nostrils are at the very tip, facing up. This allows them to breathe while hiding in the water.

Alligators eat almost anything in or near the water, including animals like raccoons and opossums that come to drink. A large alligator may grab a deer or a young bear.

Chipmunks, Squirrels, and Other Rodents

Pocket gopher

Rodents are furry animals with four front teeth that never stop growing. Rodents constantly gnaw on nuts and seeds, which wears down their teeth and keeps them from getting too long.

Chipmunk

BUSY GATHERERS

Chipmunks are small, with dark stripes on their cheeks and often also down their backs. Chipmunks gather acorns, fruits, berries, birds' eggs, and insects and store them away for the winter. They have pouches in their cheeks that allow them to stuff extra food in their mouths.

Eastern gray squirrel

The **eastern gray squirrel** makes a nest high in a tree but spends much of its time running along low branches or the ground. It often sits up on its back legs, with its paws to its mouth, chewing. Small but not shy, eastern gray squirrels will cluck loudly at a blue jay, or even at you, if they don't like how close you are getting.

Flying squirrel

Flying squirrels have flaps of skin that connect their front and back paws. They can't really fly, but they jump, then glide from tree to tree. Flying squirrels are active at night.

The **red squirrel** lives in most of the United States. It has a rusty-red back and white underside.

BURROWERS AND BUILDERS

The **groundhog** (also called a woodchuck) and the **marmot** are large, roly-poly rodents. They live in holes they dig called burrows. Their burrows have many exit holes, to help them escape if another animal tries to find them.

Pocket gophers are burrowing animals, too. The cheek pouches they use to carry food are fur lined. They can actually turn them inside out!

Beavers are natural builders. They create their own ponds by gnawing on trees until they fall. The fallen trees form a dam, which blocks the stream, creating a pond.

TAKE THAT!

A **porcupine** is a rodent with a very pointy defense mechanism. A porcupine is covered in about 30,000 sharp tubes called quills. If another animal gets too close, the porcupine will lash out with its tail. The quills will come off and stick in the other animal's body. Ouch.

Other Common Furry Animals

Some animals can live as well in cities and towns as they do in the woods. These animals may be found curled up under someone's porch or in the hollow of a tree. They will eat just about anything.

The **cottontail rabbit** has a little white tail that looks like a mushroom. It usually takes short hops. When frightened, it will hop fast in a zigzag pattern to confuse the animal that is chasing it. Cottontails are black, gray, or reddish brown on their backs, and white underneath.

The **striped skunk** is black with two fat white stripes along its back that meet at its neck. It also has a narrow white stripe down its snout. To protect themselves, skunks create and store a smelly substance near their rear ends. They spray it when another animal bothers them. (See page 66.)

FIELD FACT
Striped skunks can spray their stinky odor up to 15 feet! The stench can be smelled as far as 1 mile away.

Raccoon

Raccoons are easy to recognize. They have a black "mask" around their eyes and striped tails. They are good swimmers and tree climbers. They live almost everywhere that people do—even in New York City's Central Park.

The **opossum** is one of the strangest animals you'll see. It is the only animal in the United States that carries its young in a pouch, like a kangaroo. Opossums have hairless tails that they can use to grip things.

Opossum

ROLL OVER AND PLAY DEAD

When an opossum is scared, it falls down as if it were dead. Its body gets stiff, and it bares its teeth and gives off an awful smell. The opossum does not do this on purpose. It is a reaction to being scared, kind of like fainting. The opossum is protected because many animals will not bother something that is already dead. When a person lies down without moving, it is called playing possum.

Who's Been Here?

Raccoon prints

Once you learn to spot the clues animals leave behind, you'll know which animals are nearby—even when they are nowhere to be seen!

READ THE SIGNS

If you see a hole in the ground, it may be the home of a skunk or groundhog. If you see a tree that has had parts of its bark rubbed off, a deer may have been rubbing its antlers there.

Opossum prints

FATEFUL FOOTPRINTS

When the ground is snowy or muddy, keep an eye out for animal tracks. The tracks of opossums, raccoons, and muskrats look like small handprints.

Deer prints

Deer and moose make two-part hoofprints. (Deer prints are smaller.) When cottontail rabbits and squirrels hop, their long back feet land in front of their front feet. Their tracks look like two elongated ovals in front of two smaller circles.

Rabbit prints

THE SCOOP ON POOP

Everyone poops. But each animal poops in its own way. Cottontail rabbits leave small, round droppings. Deer make dark pellets that are flat or indented on one end and pointy on the

other. Skunk, raccoon, fox, and coyote poop, or scat, is shaped more like ours—long tubes—but not as big. You may see bones, insects, hair, seeds, or berries inside the scat. Don't touch animal droppings!

HIDDEN HOMES

Chipmunks, red squirrels, and groundhogs dig holes. Some animals borrow holes made by others. If you see a hole about 6 inches wide, with a mound of earth in front, it was probably made by a groundhog—but there could be a skunk living inside!

A large, round collection of twigs and leaves high in a tree often belongs to a gray squirrel. It is known as a drey. Other nests are home to birds. The American robin makes a cup-shaped nest of grass and mud, about 6 to 8 inches across, in the lower part of a tree or even on the ground. Hummingbird nests are incredibly tiny: about as big as a thimble. Don't collect bird nests—you don't want to prevent the birds from raising families. And old abandoned nests may be infested with pests.

Animals that hunt for their food are called predators.

Black bear

BIG, FAST, AND POWERFUL

Black bears are large. They weigh between 90 and 500 pounds. Bears sometimes hunt smaller animals, but they also eat fruits and berries, beetles and crickets, and—like Winnie the Pooh—honey.

Be cautious if you are walking in woods where bears live. Bears will not normally hurt people, but if they think you have food, they might come after it. Bears that live near people's homes sometimes go through the garbage or knock down bird feeders to eat the seeds inside.

FIELD FACT Despite their size, black bears are great at climbing trees.

Coyote

SMALL, FAST, AND POWERFUL

Have you ever heard **coyotes** howling at night? This is their way of telling each other: "Here I am." Coyotes used to live only in the western United States but have spread all over the country. They thrive in suburban neighborhoods, where they eat garbage and hunt small animals—including, sometimes, pets.

If you see a flash of red, you may have spotted a **red fox,** an animal the size of a small dog. Like coyotes, foxes are not picky eaters. They hunt mice, birds, or other small animals, and will eat fruits and even squash out of people's gardens. They are found everywhere in the United States.

Red fox

The **bobcat** is twice the size of a house cat. It has both spots and stripes, and its ears are skinny and tall. Bobcats are solitary and silent and usually avoid being noticed. But like the coyote and the fox, they live all around us.

Bobcat

DEADLY HUMANS

Bears, wolves, and mountain lions are top predators. They are so fierce that no animal can harm them. No animal, that is, except people.

Years ago, people killed most of the top predators in the United States. But laws have been passed to keep these endangered species from disappearing forever. In recent years, top predators have been growing in numbers across the United States.

Deer

Deer, moose, elk, and caribou have hooves. They eat only plants and their long legs help them run away from human hunters and wolves.

In the summer, deer eat lots of green plants.

Deer are large, graceful animals. They will stare at you for a few moments, and then leap away through the trees. Look at the deer's tail as it runs away. What color is it? The top of a **white-tailed deer**'s tail is actually brown with a dark stripe down the middle. When this deer is scared, it raises its tail high, displaying the bright white underside. This "white flag" is a sign to other deer that they should be careful, too. White-tailed deer live across much of the United States.

The western part of the country is home to another kind of deer: the mule deer. Mule deer have large ears and a black tip to their tails. The **black-tailed deer** is a kind of mule deer.

White-tailed deer

Black-tailed deer

Deer eat grass, nuts, and twigs. Their special stomachs allow them to digest tough foods like hay and bark.

In some places, there are so many white-tailed deer that the animals get into trouble. They eat farmers' crops and run onto highways, causing car crashes. Hunters help reduce the numbers of these deer.

White-tailed fawn

FIELD FACT A baby deer is called a fawn. When it cries, it sounds like a kitten.

I SPY ANTLERS!

Mule deer

Antlers fall off male deer every winter and grow again in the spring. That means there are a lot of them lying around, waiting for someone—you, perhaps—to pick them up. Searching for antlers is known as shed hunting. A tip: Look for antlers on the south side of hills, where the sun shines the most. Deer like soaking up the sun's warmth on cold winter days. Each white-tailed deer's antler has a main branch that points forward and has many smaller points jutting out. A mule deer antler forks into two main branches and may keep forking many times, forming more complex shapes.

White-tailed deer

Moose, Elk, and Caribou

Moose

Moose, elk, and caribou have hooves like deer but they are much larger. They munch on grass and plants almost constantly all summer long to store up energy for winter.

Elk

SUPERSIZE HOOVED ANIMALS

Moose live in the northern part of the United States and throughout Canada. Their antlers are wider than a deer's—more like deep shaggy bowls than branches. Unlike deer, which are shy around people, moose are easily annoyed and will sometimes charge at people or cars. The call of a moose is a deep bellow.

Elk live in the western part of the United States and western Canada. **Caribou** are sociable animals that gather in huge groups of up to 100,000. They live in Alaska and throughout most of Canada and travel long distances in the fall and spring to find the best food and living conditions.

FIELD FACT Only male deer, moose, and elk grow antlers. Both male and female caribou do.

Caribou

PHOTO CREDITS

Front Cover: Cheryl Hill/Shutterstock.com (background); Ambient Ideas/Shutterstock.com (TR); Le Do/Shutterstock.com (BR); Gastev Roman/Shutterstock.com (CL); Joshua Lewis/Shutterstock.com (BL); Doug Lemke/Shutterstock.com (TL). **Spine:** Ambient Ideas/Shutterstock.com (C). **Back Cover:** Kletr/Shutterstock.com (TL); Steve Hurst @ USDA-NRCS PLANTS Database (TC); ©iStockPhoto.com/Marcus Jones (TR); Yaro/Shutterstock.com (BL); Sergieiev/Shutterstock.com (BR). **Collecting Box:** Filip Fuxa/Shutterstock.com (leaf); Le Do/Shutterstock.com (wood texture); Cindy Hughes/Shutterstock.com (rock); Robyn Mackenzie/Shutterstock.com (note). **Interior:** 1: Le Do/Shutterstock.com (CL). 3: ©H. Stanley Johnson/Purestock/SuperStock (T); Steven Russel Smith Photos/Shutterstock.com (TR); David Davis/Shutterstock.com (CR); Tyler Boyes/Shutterstock.com (BL); Joseph Calev/Shutterstock.com (BR). 4: IRC/Shutterstock.com (CR); Melinda Fawver/Shutterstock.com (CL); Doug Lemke/Shutterstock.com (BL); Steven Russel Smith Photos/Shutterstock.com (TL). 5: Hvoya/Shutterstock.com (T); Terrance Emerson/Shutterstock.com (cottonwood); Denis Vrublesvski/Shutterstock.com (maple); Tamara Kulikova/Shutterstock.com (sweetgum); ©Dannyphoto80/Dreamstime.com (snake); Kristof Degreef/Shutterstock.com (B). **Plants and Fungi:** 7: © Mirceax/Dreamstime.com (BR); ©iStockphoto.com/Zorani (TCL); Khotenko Volodymyr/Shutterstock.com (TL); Steven Russel Smith Photos/Shutterstock.com (BCR); Petr Skarvan/Shutterstock.com (BL); ©iStockphoto.com/Stephan Hoerold (BCL); Michael Hare/Shutterstock.com (TCR); ©iStockphoto.com/Catherine Murray (TR). 8: ©iStockphoto.com/JillKyle (B); ©iStockphoto.com/Borislav Gnjidic (T); Melinda Fawver/Shutterstock.com (C). 9: Steve Hurst @ USDA-NRCS PLANTS Database (all).10: Filip Fuxa/Shutterstock.com (BL); Hypnotype/Shutterstock.com (C, TR); Le Do/Shutterstock.com (TL). 11: Rick Parsons/Shutterstock.com (BL); GoodMood Photo/Shutterstock.com (CR); Anette Linnea Rasmussen/Shutterstock.com (TL). 12: © Arquiplay/Dreamstime.com (TR); ©iStockphoto.com/Zennie (TL); J.S. Peterson @ USDA-NRCS PLANTS Database (BL). 13: ©iStockphoto.com/Missing35mm (TL); Robert H. Mohlenbrock @ USDA-NRCS PLANTS Database/USDA NRCS,1995, *Northeast Wetland Flora: Field Office Guide to Plant Species*. Northeast National Technical Center, Chester (TR); ©iStockphoto.com/Alexander Dunkel (BCR); ©iStockphoto.com/fotolinchen (BL); Shutterstock.com (TCR); Mlwinphoto/Shutterstock.com (BR). 14: U.S. Fish and Wildlife Service (CR); SlavaK/Shutterstock.com (CL); Michael P Gadomski/Photo Researchers/Getty Images (TL); Tamara Kulikova/Shutterstock.com (CR). 15: ©iStockphoto.com/Rafael Ramirez Lee (TR); Rebecca Connolly/Shutterstock.com (CL); ©iStockphoto.com/Stephan Hoerold (B). 16: USDA-NRCS PLANTS Database/Herman, D.E., et al., 1996, *North Dakota Tree Handbook*, USDA NRCS ND State Soil Conservation Committee (CL); ©iStockphoto.com/Ricky Barnard (BL); ©iStockphoto.com/DNY59 (BR). 17: J.L. Levy/Shutterstock.com (TR); © Pancaketom/Dreamstime.com (CR); Don Bendickson/Shutterstock.com (BR). 18: ©iStockphoto.com/Lurii (TR); Tamara Kulikova/Shutterstock.com (B). 19: Versh/Shutterstock.com (TR); ©iStockphoto.com/Jason Hamel (TCR); Sergieiev/Shutterstock.com (BCR); V. J. Matthew/Shutterstock.com (BR); Raif Neumann/Shutterstock.com (TL); Farrphresco/Shutterstock.com (CL); Selena/Shutterstock.com (BL). 20: USDA-NRCS PLANTS Database/Herman, D.E., et al., 1996, *North Dakota Tree Handbook*, USDA NRCS ND State Soil Conservation Committee (C); Zocchi/Shutterstock.com (BR). 21: ©Marzolino/Dreamstime.com (BR); ©iStockphoto.com/Lev Radin (BC); Stephanie Frey/Shutterstock.com (C); Ralf Neumann/Shutterstock.com (TR). 22: ©Photomother/Dreamstime.com (BR); ©Jlwhaley/Dreamstime.com (CR); Michael Hare/Shutterstock.com (TR). 23: Mary Terriberry/Shutterstock.com (TR); Timothy Epp/Shutterstock.com (TCR); Steven Russell Smith Photos/Shutterstock.com (BCR); N. Frey Photography/Shutterstock.com (B). 24: Loskutnikov/Shutterstock.com (TL); Andrew Brunk/Shutterstock.com (BL); Petr Skarvan/Shutterstock.com (CL). 25: Xuanlu Wang/Shutterstock.com (TR); ©P-squared/Dreamstime.com (CL); Igor Grochev/Shutterstock.com (TL); Susan Montgomery/Shutterstock.com (B). 26: Elena Elisseeva/Shutterstock.com (BR); Valentin Agapov/Shutterstock.com (C). 27: Rozaliya/Shutterstock.com (CR); Elena Elisseeva/Shutterstock.com (TL); Elenamiv/Shutterstock.com (CL); Marilyn Barbone/Shutterstock.com (BR). 28: Hydromet/Shutterstock.com (C). 29: withGod/Shutterstock.com (TL); Junker/Shutterstock.com (TR); Khomulo Anna/Shutterstock.com (CL); Kletr/Shutterstock.com (TCR); Raif Broskvar/Shutterstock.com (BCR); Richard Peterson/Shutterstock.com (B). 30: ©Alexeys/Dreamstime.com (C); Rusty Dodson/Shutterstock.com (BR); Steve Hurst @ USDA-NRCS PLANTS Database (BL). 31: Gurmankin/Morina/Newscom (TL); Lori Labrecque/Shutterstock.com (TR); Marekuliasz/Shutterstock.com (TCL); Andrew Williams/Shutterstock.com (BCL); ©iStockphoto.com/Michael Czosnek (CR); Cathleen A Clapper/Shutterstock.com (B). 32: iStockphoto/thinkstock (TR); Igor Plotnikov/Shutterstock.com (BL); Glinn/Shutterstock.com (CL). 33: ©iStockphoto.com/Mary Stephens (CL); D&D Photos/Shutterstock.com (TL); Sever180/Shutterstock.com (BL); Chas/Shutterstock.com (CR). 34: Mark Herreid/Shutterstock.com (BL); Stephen Ausmus/Agricultural Research Service/U.S. Department of Agriculture (TL). 35: ©Pinfoldphotos/Dreamstime.com (BR); Mike Truchon/Shutterstock.com (T). 36: Ian Lee/Shutterstock.com (TR); Kelly MacDonald/Shutterstock.com (TL); Robert H. Mohlenbrock @ USDA-NRCS PLANTS Database/USDA SCS, 1991, *Southern Wetland Flora: Field Office Guide to Plant Species*, South National Technical Center, Fort Worth. (CL); ©Kwselcer/Dreamtime.com (BL). 37: David Hughes/Photos.com (TL); ©iStockphoto.com/Alan Lagadu (BR); Michael P Gadomski/Photo Researchers/Getty Images (CL); Karloss/Shutterstock.com (CR). 38: Raif Broskvar/Shutterstock.com (BL); L. Nagy/Shutterstock.com (TR). 39: Peter Wollinga/Shutterstock.com (TR); Marie C. Fields/Shutterstock.com (CR). **Rocks and Fossils:** 41: Leonardo Viti/Shutterstock.com (TR); Tyler Boyes/Shutterstock.com (TCL, BCL); Vicspacewalker/Shutterstock.com (BR); Gracious Tiger/Shutterstock.com (TL); Jose Galveia/Shutterstock.com (TCR); jennyt/Shutterstock.com (BCR); Zacarias Pereira da Mata/Shutterstock.com (BL). 42: Peter Zurek/Shutterstock.com (BL); Tyler Boyes/Shutterstock.com (TR). 43: Tyler Boyes/Shutterstock.com (TL, CR); Kletr/Shutterstock.com (BR); Gracious Tiger/Shutterstock.com (CL). 44: Michael Baranski/Shutterstock.com (BL); jennyt/Shutterstock.com (TR). 45: Bart_J/Shutterstock.com (TR); Dr Ajay Kumar Singh/Shutterstock.com (TL); Tyler Boyes/Shutterstock.com (CL); Jose Galveia/Shutterstock.com (BR). 46: Tyler Boyes/Shutterstock.com (all). 47: Wellford Tiller/Shutterstock.com (CR); Chas/Shutterstock.com (BCR); Bortel Pavel/Shutterstock.com (CL); Carolina K. Smith, M.D./Shutterstock.com (BR); Zacarias Pereira da Mata/

Shutterstock.com (TR). **Animals:** 49: Lynn Whitt/Shutterstock.com (BL); Tom Tietz/Shutterstock.com (BCL); Elliotte Rusty Harold/Shutterstock.com (BCR); Stubblefield Photography/Shutterstock.com (TL); Kjersti Joergensen/Shutterstock.com (TCR); Steve Byland/Shutterstock.com (BR); ©iStockphoto/Simon Phipps (TR); ©Dotlock/Dreamstime.com (TCL). 50: R-photos/Shutterstock.com (CL); Andrey Pavlov/Shutterstock.com (BR). 51: NatalieJean/Shutterstock.com (TL); Alekcey/Shutterstock.com (CR); Melinda Fawver/Shutterstock.com (BR). 52: ©CathyKeifer/Dreamstime.com (BL); Hardcoreboy/Shutterstock.com (CR). 53: ©iStockphoto/Maks Dezman (CR); Melinda Fawver/Shutterstock.com (B); Smit/Shutterstock.com (TR); Yarno/Shutterstock.com (BC). 54: Steve Collender/Shutterstock.com (TR); Dean Pennala/Shutterstock.com (TL); Eric Isselee/Shutterstock.com (BL); Brian Chase/Shutterstock.com (BR). 55: Melinda Fawver/Shutterstock.com (BR); Torsten Dietrich/Shutterstock.com (CL); Mark Hodsman/Shutterstock.com (TR). 56: Animals Animals/SuperStock (BR); Joseph Calev/Shutterstock.com (BL); Jeff Grabert/Shutterstock.com (TL); Ron Rowan Photography/Shutterstock.com (TR). 57: ©iStockphoto.com/Rmarnold (TR); Cheryl Kunde/Shutterstock.com (CR). 58: Steve Byland/Shutterstock.com (BR); Caamalf/Shutterstock.com (CL); Sari Oneal/Shutterstock.com (BL). 59: Photo by Jurvetson (flickr) (BR); Jens Stolt/Shutterstock.com (TL); Steve Byland/Shutterstock.com (BL); Steve Brigman/Shutterstock.com (TR); Steven Russell Smith Photos/Shutterstock.com (CR). 60: Irin-K/Shutterstock.com (CR); Sspopov/Shutterstock.com (CL); Henrik Larsson/Photos.com (T). 61: © National Geographic/SuperStock (BR); StudioNewmarket/Shutterstock.com (CR); Argonaut/Shutterstock.com (BL); Mikhail Melnikov/Shutterstock.com (T). 62: Henrik Larsson/Shutterstock.com (TL); Dmitrijs Bindemanis/Shutterstock.com (BL). 63: ©Slambar/Dreamstime.com (BR); ©iStockphoto.com/Vassiliy Vishnevskiy (C); Doug Lemke/Shutterstock.com (BL); © Animals Animals/SuperStock (TR). 64: ©iStockPhoto/arlindo71 (BR); Joseph Calev/Shutterstock.com (CL). 65: ©Berndlang/Dreamstime.com (CR); Alexandru Axon/Shutterstock.com (B); IRC/Shutterstock.com (BR); Joseph Calev/Shutterstock.com (TR). 66: ©Heiko Kiera–Fotolia.com (CL); Guy J. Sagil/Shutterstock.com (BR). 67: ©Panama00/Dreamstime.com (B); Elena Schweitzer/Shutterstock.com (sage); Naturediver/Shutterstock.com (CL); Kesu/Shutterstock.com (basil); Dionisvera/Shutterstock.com (mint); Vlad Siaber/Shutterstock.com (magnolia). 68: Steve Byland/Shutterstock.com (BL); Martha Marks/Shutterstock.com (TL, CL). 69: Chas/Shutterstock.com (CL); Julie Lubick/Shutterstock.com (TR); Stubblefield Photography/Shutterstock.com (CR). 70: Chas/Shutterstock.com (CL); Al Mueller/Shutterstock.com (BL); Steve Byland/Shutterstock.com (TL). 71: Elizabeth Spencer/Shutterstock.com (BR); John Czenke/Shutterstock.com (TR); Brad Thompson/Shutterstock.com (CR); Steven Russell Smith Photos/Shutterstock.com (TL); Mycteria/Shutterstock.com (BR). 72: Bruce MacQueen/Shutterstock.com (CL); Steve Bower/Shutterstock.com (BL). 73: Al Mueller/Shutterstock.com (BR); Mircea Bezergheanu/Shutterstock.com (TR); Wim Claes/Shutterstock.com (C). 74: Gregory Synstelien/Shutterstock.com (CL); Bruce MacQueen/Shutterstock.com (BL). 75: Teekaygee/Shutterstock.com (CR); Dennis Donohue/Shutterstock.com (TR). 76: Takahashi Photography/Shutterstock.com (CR); Steve Byland/Shutterstock.com (TL, BL). 77: Chris Alcock/Shutterstock.com (B); Michael Woodruff/Shutterstock.com (TR). 78: Didden/Shutterstock.com (CL); FloridaStock/Shutterstock.com (B). 79: L. S. Luecke/Shutterstock.com (B); Joevoz/Shutterstock.com (TR). 80: David Davis/Shutterstock.com (B). 81: Mlorenz/Shutterstock.com (TR); Miles Away Photography/Shutterstock.com (TL); Dr. Morley Read/Shutterstock.com (CR, BR). 82: ©iStockPhoto.com/Thomas Knauer (CL); Mark Carroll/Shutterstock.com (BR); Joseph Scott Photography/Shutterstock.com (BL). 83: Christian Musat/Shutterstock.com (T); ©H. Stanley Johnson/Purestock/SuperStock (C). 84: Mike Neale/Shutterstock.com (B). 85: Bobby Deal/RealDealPhoto/Shutterstock.com (B); Steve Brigman/Shutterstock.com (CR). 86: ©iStockPhoto.com/Alexei Zaycev (BL); Steven Russell Smith Photos/Shutterstock.com (CL). 87: ©iStockPhoto.com/Jake Holmes (TR); Jerome Whittingham/Shutterstock.com (BR). 88: ©iStockPhoto.com/Marcus Jones (CR); Gerald A. DeBoer/Shutterstock.com (BL). 89: John R. McNair/Shutterstock.com (CR); MarkMirror/Shutterstock.com (TR); ©Dotlock/Dreamstime.com (BL). 90: Stefan Fierros/Shutterstock.com (BL); ©imagebroker.net/SuperStock (BR); Alex Kalashnikov/Shutterstock.com (CL). 91: Kippy Spilker/Shutterstock.com (BR); Michiel de Wit/Shutterstock.com (TR); Stolz, Gary M./U.S. Fish and Wildlife Service (CL). 92: © Minden Pictures/SuperStock (CR); James DeBoer/Shutterstock.com (BL); Melinda Fawver/Shutterstock.com (TR). 93: Cristi180884/Shutterstock.com (TR). 94: James DeBoer/Shutterstock.com (CL); Tony Campbell/Shutterstock.com (TR); Audrey Snider-Bell/Shutterstock.com (BR); Matt Jeppson/Shutterstock.com (BL). 95: iStockphoto/Thinkstock (C); Ryan Kelm/Shutterstock.com (BR); Fivespots/Shutterstock.com (TR); ©Dannyphoto80/Dreamstime.com (CR). 96: S Ansley/Shutterstock.com (BR); Kjersti Joergensen/Shutterstock.com (TL). 97: ©Imagevillage/Dreamstime.com (BR); Tony Campbell/Shutterstock.com (TR). 98: ©Designpicssub/Dreamstime.com (C); Steve Byland/Shutterstock.com (T); ©iStockPhoto.com/Walkingmoon (BR). 99: Eric Isselee/Shutterstock.com (B); Jupiterimages/Photos.com (TR). 100: Melisa Taylor/BigStock.com (TR); Steve Byland/Shutterstock.com (CL); Sharon Day/Shutterstock.com (CR); ©Gonepaddling/Dreamstime.com (BR). 101: Seawhisper/Shutterstock.com (TR); Eric Isselee/Shutterstock.com (BR); Kristof Degreef/Shutterstock.com (TCR); Fremme/Shutterstock.com (CR); ©iStockphoto/Simon Phipps (BL). 102: ©iStockPhoto.com/Geoff Kuchera (BR); Melinda Fawver/Shutterstock.com (CL). 103: iStockPhoto/Thinkstock (C); Eric Isselee/Shutterstock.com (T). 104: Emily Veinglory/Shutterstock.com (TR); Zerofische/BigStockPhoto (BR); © Minden Pictures/SuperStock (CL); Hemera Technologies/Photos.com (CR). 105: a40757/Shutterstock.com (TR); © NHPA/SuperStock (TL); Alexey Stiop/Shutterstock.com (CL); © Animals Animals/SuperStock (CR); Anne Kitzman/Shutterstock.com (BR). 106: Tom Tietz/Photos.com (BL); Nialat/Shutterstock.com (TL). 107: ©iStockPhoto.com/Eric Isselee (TR); Mlorenz/Shutterstock.com (CR). 108: ©Davidagall/Dreamstime.com (B); Christina Richard/Shutterstock.com (TL). 109: ©iStockPhoto.com/Ronald Glovan (TR); L. Powell/Shuttertock.com (CL); Tom Reichner/Shutterstock.com (BL); Pi-Lens/Shutterstock.com (CR). 110: Laubenstein, Karen/U.S. Fish and Wildlife Service (BR); Tony Campbell/Shutterstock.com (CL); ©iStockphoto.com/Paul Tessier (TL).

* Abbreviations: T=top; C=center; B=bottom; R=right; L=left.